T0129893

HONOR ROLLS

A Unique Application of Candy

NORMAN O'BANYON

HONOR ROLLS
A UNIQUE APPLICATION OF CANDY

This is a work of fiction. All of the characters, names, incidents, organizations, and dialogue in this novel are either the products of the author's imagination or are used fictitiously.

iUniverse books may be ordered through booksellers or by contacting:

iUniverse
1663 Liberty Drive
Bloomington, IN 47403
www.iuniverse.com
1-800-Authors (1-800-288-4677)

ISBN: 978-1-5320-2138-1 (sc)
ISBN: 978-1-5320-2139-8 (e)

Library of Congress Control Number: 2017905158

Print information available on the last page.

iUniverse rev. date: 04/06/2017

"I guess it all started with a gray kitten named Silvia

Seattle traffic is never pleasant. Summer Friday afternoons might be the very worst time to be in a hurry. The Toyota courtesy van had picked up a passenger at Northgate and was in route to the downtown dealership. Just before the Aurora Bridge the blue Ford in front of him hit her brakes and came to a full stop. A young woman sprang from the driver's door oblivious of the many cars that were coming to a panic stop. She was an unexpected obstacle.

"What the hell, Lady! Get back in your car for crying out loud!" He honked his horn vigorously. A couple cars behind him joined in the noise. Strangely the young woman just waved and pointed toward the curb. Her wide smile seemed incongruous to the situation.

"Get in the car fool!" he said impatiently. "Do you have a brain in that thick skull?" They were words that had been growled at him as a child.

The blue Ford driver bent down and scooped up a tiny gray kitten. She had seen the car in front of her throw the hapless creature onto the busy street without slowing down. She ran back to her car door waving the rescued feline so the other drivers could see the reason for her action. A couple drivers honked approvingly.

The van driver wasn't one of them. "Move it lady! This isn't a parking lot!"

The tiny kitten was passed to the driver's mom so they could get going again. "Mom," the driver asked breathlessly, "do you think we could keep her? Let's name her 'Reckless" because nobody collided with us."

The mom answered, "When I was a girl I had a gray kitty named Silvia. How do you know it's a girl?"

"Cause she was the only one not making a fuss that I was saving her, while those clueless men honked," the smiling young woman answered. "Golly those men were upset because I held them up for two minutes. It was the best two minutes of my day, even if you don't want to keep her."

"I once heard a pastor say in his sermon, 'Two men looked out of prison bars. One saw mud the other saw stars.' You saw a star today. Those men only saw a muddy street. I think you were marvelous to see her so quickly and to stop. We should keep her and name her Silvia."

HOW WE GOT HERE:
THE BACK-STORY

So, you think your family is screwed up; let me tell you about mine. It should make you feel better. My dad, Gerald Winter, Jerry for short, finished his second year at the Everett Vocational College in marine engines, and got a job with Maritime Marine Products, installing and repairing boat motors. His high school sweetheart, Francine, married him, a year after graduation when she was two months pregnant. That would become Michael the Magnificent. Two years later they had Christina, the perfect child. I came along three years later as an accident. They chose the name Ward for me, which means guard. They would guard against that ever happening again! I think the very first time I heard that definition I felt unwanted. The feeling got worse when they started calling me "Wart" instead.

For seven years our family rolled along pretty sweetly. In the winter, when not many people needed work on their boat, dad would come home at noon and play with us as soon as we got out of school. In the summer time we didn't get to see much of him. There was lots of work and he was able to catch up on the bills. Mom's job was cashier at a car dealership. It really was fun when Nanny Winter came to care for us when the folks weren't there. It seemed that was happening more often. I guessed she really liked having Michael and Christina around and I came along with the deal.

It was the summer after the first grade when the big fight started. Dad said mom wasn't at work when the car place was closed, and she said he wasn't sleeping at the marina either. When he found a box of Valentine cards she had been receiving from another guy, he said, "God Damn!" to mom. Now Nanny had taught us that Jesus loves us, but I guess when God damned a family it fell apart on the spot.

Dad's company offered him a better job in Bellingham and Michael wanted to go with him. Chrissy wanted to stay with mom so the three of us stayed with Nanny for a while then mom rented us a nice house of our own. It took me a long time to finally miss having Michael around. He had been pretty mean to me most of the time. Mom even let us get a puppy and a kitty from the pound place. It was different seeing dad only on his visiting days, but that wasn't too bad.

Bad started the next summer when mom asked if Nanny could keep us at her house for a weekend. Mom had a new special friend and he didn't like having kids around while they were trying to get to know each other. His name was Ralph and it didn't take long before he was way more mean to me than Michael ever was. For example, he kicked the puppy for being in his way and said he would do the same to me if I wasn't careful. Then one day I was not polite to mom and he slapped me on the side of my face hard enough to leave a hand print. Mom cried and they had a big fight. Apparently he wasn't such a special friend after all. He never came back.

Let's see, then there was Tony, who was sort of a fun guy until mom told him to keep his hands off Chrissy and there was another fight. There was Gordy who liked to smoke that stuff, you know. Both he and mom were arrested and there was plenty of concern whether Chrissy and I would be able to stay with her anymore. Finally the judge put her on probation and we never saw Gordy again.

I didn't understand the destructive spiral our family was in until Sean became mom's next special friend. He brought two big dogs with him that growled at me whenever I tried to pet them. Sean would say, "That's funny, they like normal people." In fact, he used that term a lot. When he looked in the refrigerator he might say, "That's funny. I had a fresh six pack of Bud. One's gone. You know anything about that, Wart?" Or, "That's funny. I left my smokes on the table and they are not there now. You know anything about that, Wart?" The worst time was when he said, "That's funny. I had twenty bucks in my wallet and now there is only a ten. Did you help yourself to my cash, Wart?" When I shook my head and told him I didn't know anything about his money, he grabbed my arm and the big dog jumped at me. Sean shook me like a dirty sock and I stumbled over the dog. I hit my face on the coffee table as I was falling. That's where I got this scar on my chin.

As the doctor at the hospital was stitching my injury, he noticed the red bruise on my arm and reported the signs of abuse to the police. There wasn't much of a fight this time. Sean went to jail, and so did my mom for probation violation. You know what's funny? Chrissy was the one swiping the stuff, even helping herself to mom's purse. She went to juvenile detention and I went to a temporary foster shelter. It seems the police couldn't get in touch with dad. He and Michael had moved to a new job in sunny California. Yeah, that's funny!"

The first morning at the shelter home the man of the house, I think he was a minister at the Bayview Baptist church, asked me if I had accepted Jesus Christ as my Lord and Savior. I told him that I didn't know what that meant. He took it upon himself to give me an hour-long lesson on how Jesus had gone to the cross to wipe away my sins.

"What sins," I wondered, "the sin of being born third or the sin of being born to a couple who didn't know their butt from a brick wall? Maybe it was the sin of being poor and missing out on the lessons of human decency, the sin of having no role model for being a proper son or brother. I found his lesson irritating and his righteous tone of voice intolerable. I probably shouldn't have told him that I thought his pious yapping was a crock of crap. He was mad enough to take a swing at me, so I ran into my room. Fortunately I was only there three nights, which was three nights too long.

Over the next three years I was relocated five times. Funny, they were being compensated for my lodging, my food, which was poor even compared to mom's cooking. I never understood the problem. I was small for my age so I'm sure I didn't start the fights, but there was a ton of shouting matches. I wanted them to know it wasn't the size of the dog in the fight it was the size of the fight in the dog.

The second home already had three other foster boys. I became the youngest and most picked on. They thought my nickname was funny. I was a little wart. Sometime they called me fart instead. It seemed like I did a lot of things wrong. The lazy adults thought they had a good thing going. They were receiving money for my clothes which were always from the thrift store and yet they found some reason to be upset with me and the system's payments. I think a broken door was the last straw. They told the case worker I was incorrigible, whatever that might be.

The next place was another bunch of church people who made it clear that they were doing it for Jesus. They also made it clear that I had better be thankful and learn to pray, or else. I tried to stay out of trouble, but when I started using the same words they were saying about me, I was put into detention or time out. Whatever! I think that was the one where she accused me of sneaking food from the refrigerator. She sent me back saying that I was very disobedient, and needed mental help.

Four was the group home where I shared a bedroom with three retarded kids. The woman said she was homeschooling us. What a joke, she could hardly read the book herself. I think she was trying to fool someone into thinking she was able so she could get paid more. She was dumber than a stick. When she had trouble reading a word, I started making fun of her and the other boys laughed. I'm pretty sure that was the shortest residence for me. She called me a wicked little shit and packed my clothes in a box. I ran away before the social worker got there and the police found me two days later. They put a twelve year old in Juvenile Detention for two weeks. That was wicked for sure.

Home five was probably the longest and most bazaar. Two women assured the judge that they could give me a structured and compassionate living situation. I had no choice when they were awarded custody along with the three other boys in their house. It was nice that the school bus stopped right in front of their house. It was not nice that any time we were in the bath tub one of them would walk in and gawk. They said they were making sure that we weren't jacking off. One of them made a big deal when I started to grow body hair and several inches taller. It seemed to excite them because there was more hugging and kissing between them. It seemed gross to me. When I said they were a couple queers, they said I was an irritating Wart. The big one called the social worker. They were responsible for my care yet they were quick to hand me off to someone else to try to do that. Needless to say, I was never sad about leaving any of those foster placements.

Just before I finished middle school, however, my luck changed. Steve and Lenora Hart welcomed me into their home graciously. They tried to show me that I was welcomed instead of a problem that needed to be solved even though I was pretty skeptical at first. The first sign of hope for me was when Steve said that my name was Ward and that's what they would always call me. I did find out that their son, who had been born with a bunch of challenges, had only lived a couple years. They had no other children. So I gathered that I was a stand-in substitute for the original. It might have been a bit twisted, but what the hay, it was a lot better than the last seven homes I'd been in!

Before my freshman year of high school began, I attended a summer intensive course in math and Lenora shared several video cassettes of World and U.S. History with me. She also shared several Cliff Notes booklets on literature that she was sure would be on my list of early reading. They said it might be a little challenging now but the head start would help me during the school year. They were right. For the first time in my life I didn't feel like I was in trouble or someone was mad at me. Steve also offered me an allowance so I could have some spending money and he told me of three or four jobs around the house that I could do for additional money. Sweet! He even got me a job at the car dealership he worked at; on weekends I could wash cars. The very best part was that there were no shouting matches or threats and they never mentioned going to church once.

The summer before my junior year, when I got my license, I was a dealership shuttle driver and on occasion I worked on the sales floor. Steve told me with genuine appreciation that I had a gift for communication. I even sold a few cars, receiving a super commission.

Seattle traffic is never pleasant. Summer Friday afternoons might be the very worst time to be in a hurry. I had just picked up a passenger at Northgate and was in route to the downtown dealership. Just before the Aurora Bridge the blue Ford in front of me hit her brakes and came to a full stop. The young woman sprang from the car oblivious of the many cars she was blocking.

'What the hell, Lady! Get back in your car for crying out loud!' I shouted. I honked the horn vigorously. A couple cars behind me joined in the noise. Strangely the young woman waved and pointed toward the curb. "Get in the car fool!" I said impatiently. "Do you have a brain in that thick skull?" It's funny how abusive words from my past now were aimed at others.

The blue Ford driver bent down and scooped up a tiny gray kitten. She had seen the car in front of her throw the hapless creature onto the busy street without slowing down. She ran back to her car door waving the rescued feline so the other drivers could see the reason for her action. A couple drivers honked approvingly.

I wasn't one of them. "Move it lady! This isn't a parking lot!"

It was a great summer job, and I didn't have any accidents or other incidents or people shouting at me.

My grades were not stellar the first year, but the second year showed marked improvement, as did the third year. My straight A grades for my senior year caused my school counselor to give me a list of possible scholarship sources. He advised me to apply to several. "These are all small grants, but who knows what might work for you?" he said. For once I didn't think it was an effort at a funny remark. He really believed in me. I've never been very athletic, so no sports program was interested in me. Nor have I been one to socialize, so popularity was of no assistance. Girls were an irritating puzzle and I had few close friends. I didn't see the point and I didn't expect much assistance either.

Steve and Nora, however, were more support than I could ever imagine. They acknowledged that the foster system took me only to my eighteenth birthday. But they wanted me to know that this was my home and they would give me assistance as long as I needed it. Steve also told me that the Rotary Club, where he was an officer, had a generous student scholarship program, and promised to provide the necessary application information.

As it turned out I received three local scholarships plus the Rotary scholarship to attend the Community College. The four would pay for my tuition and books. If I lived at home I would accumulate no debt. Two years hurried by and I was awarded an AA Associate Degree and an invitation to give the gratitude speech to the Rotary club.

"Mister President, officers and members of Rotary International, welcome guests, if you can imagine how nervous I am to be before you today, you can try a little harder to imagine how much more I am grateful for your generous assistance I have had during my two years of academic training." A chuckle of laughter eased them into the prepared speech. "With your generosity, I have successfully concluded my work at the Community College with a 4 point grade average in liberal studies." Now there was a generous applause. "I will not bore you with details of the challenges. Those members of this organization who are aware of the hurdles that had to be cleared in the past six years can appreciate even more my success. Today I am here to salute your faith in me, to acknowledge your foresight and courage.

"Perhaps you were watching the news a couple nights ago when a brave team of Marine Biologists set off from Santa Monica to rescue a whale that had become entangled by some fish trap ropes. The lines had so tightened around the huge animal that they were sure it would not survive without assistance. The camera followed the little Zodiac as it maneuvered alongside the whale in distress. Again and again they tried to loosen the line, to hook the offending ropes. I held my breath both in anxiety for the animal and admiration for the skill of those offering aid. Would they succeed before the frightened animal dove for the depths in fear possibly to lose its life, to die from no fault of its own? Did it understand that their efforts were in its best interest?

"To my relief the sharp blade cut first one and then the other offending ropes and the whale was freed. It could now proceed north to the icy waters of Alaska to feed on Krill, to get fat and pregnant. It was free to swim the depths. In a moment of clarity I realized I had been watching a metaphor of my own academic endeavor.

"Snared by poverty and encumbered by a tangle of dysfunctional parents, I had those two possibilities of education, slim and absolutely none at all. But thanks to your courage and foresight, thanks to your compassionate generosity, thanks to Rotary International's standard to always lend assistance, my journey may now continue. Because of this tremendous beginning, there are those who believe I can go further. Central University has accepted my transfer as a junior to work on a Bachelor of Arts degree in Education. And following that achievement we will acquire a Master's, with the intent of teaching High School Math. However daunting the future might be, however challenging, ladies and gentlemen, it will be attainable because you helped cut the ropes! Your facilitating scholarship has allowed me to plumb the depths of learning and set sights on far distant goals. Today I feel as that whale must; I am free. Hear me as I whisper 'Thank you ever so much.' Or I shout from the rooftop, 'Thank you, Thank you, Thank you.' It can't be said enough: Thank you!" Applause filled the room as smiling people stood, some wiping tears from their eyes. Steve Hart was understandably the most energetic and proud.

To my recollection that was the first time I had ever heard an ovation for me! I breathed it in; I drank it deeply. And when I completed the Bachelor degree from Central I heard the sound again. While it may have been for the entire graduating class, I surely claimed my share of the enthusiastic praise.

Steve was so enthused about my accomplishments he submitted my name to the Rotary committee that was planning the national conference in Chicago. I was stunned when he told me I could make the whale speech again; this time to more than three thousand delegates. I was far more nervous speaking to such a huge gathering and the applause was ten times more thrilling. Before we left the Windy City Steve and Nora took me to the Comedy Klub for an evening of stand-up comedy. I was amazed that simple stories about a person's personal life could be so entertaining. We laughed all evening, even when the potty-mouth girl made references to her sexual skills that were inappropriate. Nora was the most offended, and yet she laughed longer than the others around us. It was an interesting night that would have a lasting effect on me.

The Harts agreed that a break before engaging the Master's program would be a good idea. If I wanted to work at the dealership, I could build a bit of a nest-egg. They also put me in touch with the social worker who had arranged my placement with them. She gave me little help in trying to get in touch with my parents or siblings. After parole, mom had moved out of the state, leaving no forwarding address. Chrissy had been in court ordered rehab on two occasions and was serving a sentence at Monroe. The case-worker had no idea where my dad was, but Michael was in Texas State prison in Huntsville serving a fifteen year sentence for drug trafficking. At first I wanted to get on a plane; Steve and Nora even offered to go with me so we could all go on down to Corpus Christi for a little bit of spring break sunshine. But then reality kicked in and I asked myself what I would even want to say to him. The last time he saw me was when I was in the first grade. What would I expect from him? Certainly not a reunion hug and compliments for graduating from college. I decided to work in the dealership and try to earn enough to buy a better car.

In many ways it was an idyllic year. Using my Central counselor's syllabus I read six of the required books. The Harts presented me with both a laptop computer and an iPad to help take notes. Nora gave me a new smart phone and said she would pay for the contract if I would promise to call home at least once a week while I was in school. I found a very nice furnished cottage in Ellensburg. With my new gold Mazda sport coupe I felt every bit the prepared graduate student.

Twelve weeks of accomplishment into the fall quarter were completed before I finally ran into the day Theresa met me in the student center. She was darling and so short she made me feel tall. Her blue tights and grey dress could have been straight out of a fashion magazine. Suddenly my turkey sandwich lost its flavor.

"You're in Larson's Advanced Calc class," she announced as if I had forgotten.

"Yeah, I'm Ward Winter," I managed to get out around the bite I was chewing.

Before I could ask her name, she said, "Of course you are. By any chance are you going to Dr. Charles' open house this evening? I'm Theresa and I'd sure appreciate a ride."

The school's Vice President traditionally offered the graduate students a social opportunity to get into the Thanksgiving spirit. I had not intended to trade an evening of study for a pointless gathering, but looking into her brown eyes I had a sudden urge to change my plans. "Of course I would be honored. Where do you live?"

"I'll be in front of Kappa Sig house at 7:00 o'clock. If it is still raining, I'll be under a pink umbrella so please don't be late." She stroked my shoulder and said, "Thanks for the rescue." Just like that she turned and walked away. I was pretty impressed. If I had known how the evening would end I would have found a rock to hide under.

I made sure I was on time, maybe even a minute or two early. There she was looking even smaller in the dark and very vulnerable. She slid into the car with only a brief thanks for being prompt. Conversation was sparse, pretty much focusing on finding the hilltop street and empty lot that was being used as a parking place. There must have already been three dozen cars there. I thought she was being helpful by pointing out that there were several parking spots in the back corner. I was unaware that like a lamb I was being led to disaster.

As we got out of the car there were three young men in some sort of argument. The one nearest said, "Jimmy thinks it will take two, but I think one will be enough. What do you think?" He didn't seem to be addressing anyone in particular, but the question was scarcely finished when the baseball bat in his hand slammed against my hip. The pain was like nothing I had ever experienced. My body was rigid and I shouted, "What the hell?" I couldn't move, or think.

"Damn, Jimmy, you were right," he said in mock surprise. Then I was struck from behind. The blow landed just above my ear and my world turned pitch black. I don't remember falling or having my keys, wallet and cell phone pulled from my pockets. Through a rumble I heard someone say, "Come on Terry, hop in." Apparently she did because I was bleeding alone in the dark in excruciating pain and confusion until another car came in to park. Fortunately for me they called 911 and help was on its way.

Two police officers were trying to get information from me while the EMTs were securing me to a backboard. I gave them the license plate on the Mazda and the address of my place. I also said that the Harts could verify that information and then I guess I passed out because the next thing I remember I was in the hospital. I was able to describe the three boys as Asian. When I considered it a bit more so was Theresa, if that was really her name. Then, finally, I was given a shot of pain relief. Thank goodness I didn't need to dwell on this horrific thing for a while.

In the morning Steve and Nora were beside my bed. With a shaved head, a scalp full of staples, a body cast with my leg elevated, I looked and felt like a total mess. Nora stroked my shoulder and said, "When life is tough you must remember that you are tougher. I know that is a challenge right now, but it is the absolute truth."

First we listened to the doctor explain that I had a skull fracture and a severe concussion. A steel plate had been inserted and seven staples had been used to close the gash which would produce the new scar that looks like a permanent part in my hair. My femur was fractured as was the pelvis surrounding the hip socket. Surgery to attach another plate and several screws strengthened the fragile joint. I would need to be in a cast for at least a month. That would be a lot of bed pans, but she had declared that I am tougher.

Then we listened to the police officer report that the cottage had been pretty much cleaned out. They got away with my iPad, and worse, my laptop with a Master's thesis and several written class assignments. I asked him about the briefcase under the desk. That had all my important papers including banking information and the title to the Mazda. He said there was very little of value left in the house. The officer reported that my debit card had been used in a Cheney food market and gas station. The security cameras identified a Vietnamese family. How damned disappointing. The whole thing seemed so unfair. Every time my life seemed to be going somewhere some gigantic screw-up came along and kicked it to the curb. I would scream but what good would that do? No one would listen or care. The assault triggered feelings of abuse and neglect from my childhood and reawakened terrible resentment.

Let me just cut to the bottom line. The Trans, including Theresa who was the ring leader, all went to prison charged with felony assault and grand theft felony. It wasn't the only time they had pulled such a robbery stunt, just the only time there was evidence against them. That's two strikes; one more and its Life! The Mazda was auctioned off in Las Vegas before we could reclaim it; and I lost all my debit deposit as well as the computers. The owner of the cottage kept the last month's payment and damage deposit to replace his lost inventory. I'm the guy who took it in the shorts again! I'm in a cast and screwed out of a year of grad school! The only good thing that had ever made a difference in my life had been dashed by a pack of ruthless thieves that didn't have a flicker of humanity. Go figure! All because I wanted to give a good looking chick a ride to the open house!

O.K. to be fair, the Hart's Homeowner and car insurance made a significant settlement. my medical expenses were paid by the University because I was a student at a sanctioned event And I was given credit for the academic work I had done. Fortunately a thumb drive with my work copied on it was missed by the Trans. It only took an extra year to accomplish my academic goals on line. That was also a year of physical therapy and rehab. I lost about twenty pound that I didn't know was excess. That new trim body also looked better with hair long enough to cover the scar on my head. I'm once again overwhelmed by the Hart's generosity and compassion. During that healing time attorneys were working on the Tran family to realize some sort of righteous reimbursement for the damages. They had a large farm and deep pockets. When the judge put a lien on them and also charged them with my attorney's fees and on-going medical expenses the dust settled; the attorneys made out best but I did have enough to start over.

In June of 2001 I was granted a Masters Degree in Education with a major thesis in Mathematics, but it didn't amount to a damned thing to me. I felt that everything important to me, my innocent optimism, cheerful trust in others, hope for a bright future had been lost, forcibly taken from me. How damned sad; I was twenty eight years old, single and still hobbling around with a crutch, homeless as well as unemployed, and on top of it all, I hated women. I was afraid of the dark and groups of people frighten me too. I felt like a rat in a maze.

I worked in the dealership for a year feeling sorry for myself. Then things began to get better. Maybe my head was finally healing. The takeaway lesson I learned was that it is not time that heals all wounds, but love. The Harts will forever be my champions.

The Spokane Valley district called me to teach algebra at Joel E. Harris High School. It reminded me that I hadn't lost everything; an education may be the most important treasure of all. It's too bad I didn't consider the importance of a positive attitude as well, or realize the results of my anger.

With the settlement money I purchased an old farmhouse in the west valley. It was big and cheap, in need of a lot of TLC. I drove to San Francisco to pick up a rescue dog named Frannie Pants. She was a Cane Corso, which we call an Italian Mastiff. Fawn with a black mask and a gray muzzle with a lot of abuse in her past. We were a pair of victims. I was advised that she had a limited life expectancy, but she was a constant companion as long as she got TLC too. Fortunately summers were available for me to do a lot of that and it seemed therapeutic to my attitude. The farmhouse became a reflection of my return to humanity. Before long, with some modern improvements and stylish embellishment, the old place was an impressive home, and the Harts had a reason and place to visit me.

The dangerous thing about responsibility is that it very easily may become abusive. I accepted the job without consideration for the people I was there to assist. I suppose from the very beginning the die of failure was cast. Grading algebra was pretty basic. The answer was either correct or wrong; the student understood the principle or he didn't. They either passed or failed. And many failed. The sad part of that was I didn't think it was my problem, or the result of my negligence.

I had two meetings with Mr. Standard the Principal who was trying to motivate me to care about those students who were failing. I countered with the idea that if they might spend as much time in homework as they were in sports they might receive substantially better grades. Mr. Standard tried to impress upon me that my role as teacher included motivating the students to try harder. There was a considerable part of the classes that failed and would need to repeat it next year, or take the night class for adults which would substitute for a passing grade. I received an unfavorable first year evaluation.

Toward the end of my second year, there was a mom who took considerable exception with my inflexible attitude. Her daughter had failed last year and was well on the way to repeating. I tried to explain to her that the information was in the textbook and the instructions were clear to other students. I couldn't hold the hand of students who chose not to try. She called me Napoleon, because I had a little man attitude. Granted I was only 5' 10" and weighed 140, but she was making it so personal. She also filed a complaint with both Mr. Standard and the District Superintendent. I was given the option of termination or a referral to apply for an opening at Roosevelt High School in the Seattle District. There is no way to sugar-coat failure and there is no other word that could more accurately describe my teaching attitude than that I was a failure for sure. With two unacceptable evaluations, the

Seattle School District put me on probation for a year to have a series of tests and refresher classes. I was glad to work at the dealership again to earn a bit of spending money.

When the farmhouse sold I received five times what I had paid for it. As much as I had done to fix it up, I really expected to enjoy living there a while. It was just another disappointment in a never ending string. My deepest sorrow was that one afternoon when I got home I found that Frannie's heart finally gave out; she was dead in her bed. I sat on the porch bawling like a baby. Could life get any more crappy for me? I left her ashes at the farm. She had been a great friend during a challenging brief time. I loaded my stuff in boxes and rented a U Haul trailer and moved to expensive, noisy, smelly, crime-ridden, traffic-snarled, disappointing Seattle. Perhaps losing Frannie was the jolt at the bottom of the pit that put me on the path to sensibility. Prices were so high in Seattle that I could only purchase another seventy year old fixer-upper, a daylight basement near Green Lake. It was large, full of potential and ideally located to Roosevelt High School and downtown Seattle. In a moment of clarity I understood that I had to find a more civil attitude and a gracious teaching track.

Something happened while I was on probation. I wish I could tell you that it was easy. There were some moments that I simply wanted out, totally! I knew the blame was mine and a fresh attitude would be up to me as well. So, I have been here a full year evaluating my life and trying to learn how to find my soft side and learn courtesy; I must communicate with uninspired kids, which brings us up to date.

ROOSEVELT CHANGE

Walking down the morning hallway Ward stood out wearing his gaudy green and gold plaid jacket. He intended to be noticed.

"Good morning Mr. Winter. I like your jacket." A smiling young man groaned.

"No you don't Michael. The last time I wore it you said it looked like something from Thrift Center." The response was cheery and fun.

"I was just trying to be polite," the passing observer said. "Its way worse than that." Both laughed at his humor.

A girl giggled, "Cool jacket, Mr. Winter. That's Roosevelt spirit!"

Ward answered loudly, "I've got spirit! Yes I do!"

From down the hall they heard another female voice join in saying, "I've got spirit! How about you?" It was a pleasant way to get the Autumn Monday of fall classes started. He received several more similar comments before he turned into his classroom.

When the buzzer sounded he made sure that each student had their textbook. He spent a few minutes talking about the importance of algebra not only because it was a requirement for graduation, but more important, it was the springboard into deeper math sciences. "So, let me introduce you to the simple plan for the next twelve weeks. In your textbook there are forty four one page reading assignments. Each page is followed by four exercises that will make clear the theme for the day. Every class will be a time when we grade each other's homework. Your grade for the quarter will be an aggregate of your homework. No tests or other papers and I do not grade on a bell curve. If it should happen that you all ace this class, you will all receive an A with my hilarious praise. Are you getting the picture? It's pretty easy as long as you remain current. I'll warn you that if you get behind it is very difficult to catch up. If you do not pass this class you must take it over until you do. For me that means job security." There was a mild groan from the class. "Remember, It is a graduation requirement. No joke."

"Now one more thing. We don't need to do an exercise tonight. Instead I want you to view the video entitled 'Stand and Deliver.' I'll bet some of you have already seen it. It really is a good flick. Obviously there will be nothing to grade tomorrow, so I want you to answer these two questions about the film: what is the name of the real life teacher? Not the actor. And what made the class turn around? Our library has a couple dozen videos for you as does the Roosevelt Video on the corner of 75th.

"As we talk about the film tomorrow I am going to write a grade in our attendance book next to your name based on your answers. At the beginning of week ten I'm going to give you the opportunity to receive either the grad I have written or the aggregate of all your exercises. Do you understand what I am saying? Think about that a bit. It might be a really good deal, or none at all."

Anticipating the end of class buzzer, he began to put on the garish jacket, saying, "Yes, I've heard most insults about that garment. The most often asked is, 'Where did you buy that, and more importantly why did you?' I will tell you that it is more a tool to allow us to speak to one another than any fashion statement. This morning I give it an A plus. Let's see how we do tomorrow." The buzzer sounded and the first class shuffled out. That happened three more times before the afternoon was over.

Ward was in the faculty room filling out his daily report. Three more math teachers entered. "There he is; the man of the hour," Greg Jefferson announced. "We were just talking about you, Ward. How do you do it?"

Grinning widely he answered, "That's a trick question, right? The correct answer is, seldom, cautiously and discretely. Did I get one out of three right?" They all chuckled together.

Sean Foster, the youngest one of the four said. "Come on. We want to know on the first week of classes how you already have students telling us, 'That's not the way Mr. Winter does it.' Or we hear, 'We are lucky to be in Mr. Winter's class.' Or, 'Mr. Winter said…' You sound like a frigging rock star. What's your secret?"

His first thought was gratitude that he was not failing again. "Gentlemen, you are embarrassing me," Ward said with a shake of his head. "There is no magic to teaching algebra." When the other three snorted their non-agreement, he continued, "I use 90% textbook, one percent courtesy and 9% playfulness, which is the universal language of teenagers. The other half is I try not to bore them, knowing that I will most of the time anyway."

"You seem to be doing something right," one of the fellows said. "I don't hear those positive compliments given to other faculty. Are you bribing them?"

"Jay, will you promise not to tell on me?" He glanced around furtively as though someone might be listening. "Tomorrow when we have our quiz, everyone who has a correct exercise will get a Tootsie Roll." Ward hadn't thought about doing that until just this moment. But what a great idea. He would get a couple bags of the Minnie ones on his way home. The conversation switched to more routine topics until they were ready to leave.

"Hey Ward, we're going to Giggles next Thursday evening. Will you come along? Who knows, with your charm at the table, we might get lucky."

"That's funny," Ward replied with a wide smile. "I've never been invited to be a seduction totem." When the hooting stopped he said seriously, "Sorry, I have a date. Every evening I take a walk with Frannie. She loves to see the other folks out having a good time around the lake." It was, of course misinformation because all he had of Frannie were tender memories. But these guys didn't know that.

A month later their number had grown by one as Sam Lawrence, the Biology teacher, joined the group of single males. Once again Jay Taylor asked, "Ward, Buddy, we're going to Giggles again Thursday night. They have an open mike from 7 to 8. It's a real hoot. Since its raining, you probably won't take Granny out for her walk. Will you join us?"

Laughing, Ward replied, "Jay, you wing nut, I didn't say I was walking Granny. I had an Italian Mastiff named Frannie." He over pronounced the name for clarity. "She weighed more than you and needed exercise, but not as much as you do." When the laughter settled down he added, "She's gone now, so yeah, I can join you for a bit, but I must warn you that I don't drink and I have a nasty aversion to big crowds."

Sam leaned in closer and asked, "Is there a reason for that? Did something cause that aversion?" His steady gaze indicated a genuine caring.

Quietly changing the mood, Ward answered, "Yeah, In graduate school I was attacked by a group of hooligans with baseball bats. I lost everything including a year of grad school. It took about two years to heal and I can't pass through a metal detector without showing my doctor's permission slip." His voice was soft with the recollection of old memories.

Sam asked one more tender question. "Is that why you had a mastiff for a pet; was she your guardian?"

In that moment Ward was aware that he and Sam would always be great friends. He answered, "Yup. She was the only woman in my life, and the only one that ever will be."

The common thought with the other four at the table was a question of Ward's sexual orientation. Was he saying that he was gay? Before they left the room, Jay shared that the subject for Thursday's open mike would be about politics. "What would you do to fix Washington?"

Ward was embarrassed and would never publically admit that for the next three evenings he thought of little else than that question. How would you fix Washington? But he was relatively sure that he would not need to stand before a half drunken audience to try to answer it. He had been given the rules. There are twenty two tables in the room. By drawing, ten of them would be chosen for stand-up. That was a fifty-fifty split. Each table would choose which member would be given the microphone. That was a five to one odds.

STANDUP DISASTER

"Ward, Ward, Ward," the four collaborators chanted as their fists beat time. "Ward, Ward, Ward!" It seemed the probability wasn't that remote after all.

When the microphone was handed to him, the M.C. said, "Ward, the topic is how would you fix Washington and the floor is yours."

Ward greeted the crowd and asked them to help him stomp the crap out of the other four wienies at his table. After a tiny bit of laughter, he asked, "Did you hear that Barnum and Bailey is going out of business? Yeah, it seems that all the clowns are going to work in Washington." There was perhaps a bit more laughter.

"The question of how we would fix Washington, at least asks the right people for an answer, because we are the ones who have allowed this mess to happen. Every vote cast has made a difference and those uncast made even greater change. In the beginning there were three arms of government that balanced one another. Each was dependent on the other two. The Executive branch made nominations that congress could approve and judicial could make into law. It was like making a good cocktail, a bit of mixer, some bourbon and ice. We have allowed the drink to become too big and it has spilled all over the bar."

Someone in the back called out, "That's not funny!"

Ward pointed toward the speaker and said, "Your darned right it isn't. Politicians have become rich lifelong club members. We have allowed Political Action Committees and super pacs to fund special interest factions that have given our congressional process constipation."

Someone at the back shouted, "Give him the hook!"

As though he didn't hear the interruption, Ward continued, "And we have come to believe that it is America's responsibility to protect every other worldly faction from itself. That has cost us three thousand American lives in Iraq, and eight thousand lives in Afghanistan, and in the past year over fifty trillion dollars. And that is only one small part of the globe we are protecting."

Someone else cried out, "Oh please be done."

But he bravely continued, "I've only got one more minute, so let me suggest that we treat Washington like an ICU case; we quarantine the hell out of it. We kick out all the pacs and groups that are trying to influence government with their big dollars. The only people that should be in Washington are part of the original three arms. We treat the cancer by not allowing it back into the body. We purge all the lifers by electing only trained rookies; no incumbents, regardless of how cute they are. Isn't it funny that the very party which nominated Abraham Lincoln is the same one that nominated Ronald Reagan, a Hollywood actor!

"Whoops, there went my red light. Next time I'd like to tell you about my love life. Now that is something to giggle about. Thanks for the open mike."

A man who had been very efficient at getting the serving person's attention, tossed the last of his beer toward the speaker. He growled, "Jerk the Jerk! Show Mr. Buzz-kill the way out." When those around him tried to ease his outburst, he shouted even louder, "I came in here to laugh not be put to sleep by a wimpy Democrat!" He tossed some napkins toward the stage and a confused Ward who was accepting the tirade made his way back to his table murmuring, "Thanks a lot guys. Sure let's get Ward to stand up. He's really funny".

The room was quiet. Groaning was the only sound made by those who were trying to make sense of his lecture. There certainly weren't any giggles.

"Come on, Let's hear it for the Professor,' the M.C. encouraged. "Maybe he didn't make you giggle, but he is sure making you think! Let's give the newbie a warm hand." There was a tiny bit of courteous clapping without enthusiasm.

"O.K" the M.C. tried to change the mood in the room by using a more positive voice, "let's hear it from table ….. sixteen." A bright light illuminated a table at the other side of the room. As a young woman stood up. The M.C. chuckled, "It's Florence from Puyallup. Come on up Florence!" She was apparently a regular at Giggles.

As soon as she received the microphone Florence said in that surprised tone of voice, "Oh my God, there is a town trying to steal our name? That's not fair. How could they ever think we wouldn't find out about it and take it back? They are going to be in such trouble. They probably don't get enough rain to keep their lawns green so they are trying to trick the clouds into giving them some." There was a chuckle that rippled humorously. "Everybody knows it rains all the time in Washington."

Changing to a confidential whisper, she went on. "I heard there are lots of statues and monumental things with great big buildings where they make speeches and rules and vote. Yeah, really! Oh my God, I heard there are ten times more men there than women. Think about that girls! You could score every night if you wanted too, whatever your waistline or small breasts!" Her happy expression turned to a frown. "But then their wife would probably find out and there would be a scandal." She shook her head, but immediately switched back into that bright happy voice. "But then Hollywood would make it into a miniseries and you would become rich and famous with a blue dress!" She put her hand on the side of her face.

"You know, I was going to go there when I graduated. Then one of my friends told me it was one of the most dangerous cities in the country. There is more than one murder a night there. Well sure, what would you expect with all those men fighting for those lucky girls. They shoot one another in the streets and alleys. Well wait, they probably shoot them in the heart or head if they are murdered. I heard about a man who was in the operating room after being shot. The doctor was having trouble because the bullet was in him yet. Can you tell me where's him's yet is and how big is it?" she said with raised eyebrows. She shrugged at the groans for a silly joke, then acted startled to get back to what she had been saying. "I just meant they didn't shoot them in the bedroom. Because if they were in the bedroom, Oh my God, they wouldn't be thinking about murder now, would they? Of course not!" She did a graceful pirouette followed by three pelvic thrusts.

Her light turned yellow. "Oh my God, we all know what that means. When I'm in the car that means go faster." Speaking as rapidly as she could, Florence concluded, "Washington. is.the.place. where.ordinary.people.go.to.become.famous. They. don't. need.to.be.rich.but.will.always.get.rich.there." She took a loud breath and concluded, "If.I.can.make.it.here.at. Giggles. I.think.I.could.make.it.big.time.in.Washington. Thanks.for. listening.to.me." Breathlessly she slumped as the room was filled with applause. The five at Ward's table seemed most enthusiastic.

Instead of returning to table sixteen, however, Florence followed Ward to his table, and squeezed in beside him hunkering without a chair. "I want to tell you," she whispered in a hushed voice, "that I thought you were terrific. Yeah, I know you didn't get folks to laugh, but darn, you had a lot to say! Are these the wienies you want me to stomp the crap out of?" Offering her hand in greeting she went around the table. When she got to Ward she didn't let go. "I thought you showed a lot of courage to hang in there and try. And I thought the humor you shared was too intelligent for this lubricated crowd. 'Congressional constipation' should have had them laughing out loud. I don't want you to give up. I want to hear more from you, so will you promise me you'll come back?

We're here every Thursday, and the whiners I'm with always make me the lamb for slaughter. Please promise me you'll be back." Her eyes searched his until she released his hand and stood up. Before she left she asked the others at the table, "Will you feebs bring him back next Thursday and sit near us? I'd like to hear about his love life and get to know you all."

As she walked away Jay glanced to make sure she was out of earshot before quietly saying, "Damn Ward, how do you do it? You are a seduction totem! As a comedian you are a train wreck. But you scored an entire table of women for us! That is so much greater than a few laughs." He reached over and gently punched Ward's shoulder.

As soon as Ward got home he called Steve even though it was a bit after nine. He needed to tell someone about the colossal mess he had been as a stand-up comic.

After listening attentively, Steve said, "Buddy, don't be so hard on yourself. That M.C. should know better than ask a mathematician to solve a problem. You did a sensational job as requested. Don't you remember when we were at the Comedy Klub, no one had anything practical to talk about. They told us a bunch of silly trivia using silly voices, bad language and personal opinions. The humor was in their discourse and timing. You went right at the core of our political problem, which is not funny however we look at it. It's sad and you were brave to call all of it to their attention.

Steve chuckled and said, "Next time, tell them that their current break-up is nothing to be sad about. It took you two years to get over your break up," Steve paused before adding, "because she used three bad brothers and a baseball bat. It's not funny, but it's good stand-up."

Ward was glad that he had called, and more grateful for Steve's wisdom.

The next morning Ward had finally managed to quit thinking about the disappointing evening when a girl in his second period class raised her hand.

"Yeah, Ginger, do you have a question?" He wondered what she might want.

The young lady asked, "Mr. Winter, did you do stand-up at Giggles last night?"

The teacher was caught off guard and at first was tempted to deny his activities, but realized that would bring even more trouble, so he simply said, "Yeah, four other faculty guys were with me." He hoped that would satisfy the question.

It didn't, for she said, "My folks were there. I guess you were not properly introduced but the M.C called you 'Professor.' Someone told my mom you were a teacher here at Roosevelt. This morning she wanted me to ask around," Ginger held up a business card, "and give this to you. "She is chairman of the Republican Windermere Caucus. She would appreciate chatting with you. She said you were terrific, even though nobody laughed." Ginger brought the card and laid it on his desk obediently.

Ward wished she had not hung that last sentence out there. Now he and the whole class were thinking about the dismal truth that nobody laughed. But to maintain the tenuous connection with his students, he promised that he would give her mom a call later.

"Good evening Mrs. Jameson, I'm Ward Winter, King of Stand-up when I'm not teaching at Roosevelt."

The lady on the other end of the line chuckled and answered, "Now that's funny. First of all, please call me Peggy. I feel like I already know you because Ginger has been talking about you since the start of school. Before we get into anything else, I want to thank you for rescuing a student who was suffering from low self-esteem and lack of motivation. She has spoken about you in glowing terms. She said you started the year by asking them not to do any homework, but to watch an inspiring video. We all enjoyed it." She paused a moment as though collecting her thoughts.

"She also told us that you have an unusual teaching style that depends on their involvement with the daily exercises. Do you actually toss Tootsie Rolls to those who correctly answer the questions?"

"Well, I do," he admitted. "But they are the mini ones and I don't imagine they will ruin their lunch appetites or hurt them if they fail to catch it."

"Ward, you have found a way to make positive reinforcement instant and shared by their peers. I think that is brilliant. I just wish my algebra teacher had been as playfully insightful." There was another long pause. "I can see why you were not appreciated by the Giggles crowd, half of whom were already a couple drinks into too many, and the other half haven't a clue how our government works. Bob and I were seated way at the back so we didn't have a chance to meet you. But we listened and knew that you are a person we want on our social calendar. May we invite you to brunch some Sunday? I have a couple couples that I would love to introduce to you. Can we find an available date?"

Ward smiled as he pondered, "Let's see, I think you are referring to my calendar, and not my social life? Oh wait, there is none of either! Any Sunday before the holiday break is good for me."

She said she would be delighted if he could bring a guest. She would check with the friends and get back to him.

A NEW BEGINNING

On Thursday Jay and Ward arrived at Giggles before the other three guys and two of the ladies. They were eager to find an available parking space in the busy University district. Florence expressed delight in the presence of the guys and introduced Caroline, Frieda, and Sarah. Then she orchestrated a merging of the two tables by seating the three ladies at table fifteen to reserve it and asked the two fellows to be seated at sixteen.

"Only if you guarantee I will be excused from being the human sacrifice if sixteen is drawn," Ward said sternly. "I have learned there is precious little difference between the words laughter and slaughter."

Florence said happily, "There's that intelligent humor I so appreciate. We're really glad you guys are here." That brought a chuckle from the others. In only a few minutes Maria and Becky arrived and were introduced. When the other three guys came in they understood the seating rearrangement, and heartily approved it although they didn't show their delight. Ward's secret talent was at work.

When introductions were complete the men were surprised to hear that all eleven of them were in the Seattle school system. Maria and Sarah were middle school teachers; Carolyn taught at Nathan Hale High School; Florence, who really wasn't from Puyallup, was the principal at Exstein Middle School; Becky was a counselor for the district and Frieda was head of the teacher's union.

Ward asked if they truly wanted a smattering of common teachers to be seen in the same prominent crowd. He was assured that his honor would be protected. It was a pleasant way for the evening to begin. Apparently Florence had some influence with the M.C. for neither table fifteen or sixteen were called to the microphone so there was ample opportunity to chat. She was also the big sister to table sixteen because the other ladies deferred to her leadership. Ward couldn't remember a more enjoyable evening.

That must have been a fairly unanimous experience for in the following week there were several notes and phone calls exchanged to express appreciation and eagerness for a continuation. The next Thursday Becky asked if she could be seated next to Ward. She had a professional question to ask him.

When it was obvious that the other folks at the table were engaged in conversations, Becky leaned closer to Ward and said, "Last week I noticed that you had two cokes to drink. I don't want to offend you so may I ask if you are in a recovery program or have some allergy."

For just a second Ward considered the possibility that he might be a totem after all. There was no other reason for such a lovely lady to request the chair next to his. Her short curly brown hair accentuated a charming face that was looking directly into his eyes. She seemed graceful and athletic at the same time. Although this was their first meeting, he felt like they had been together before. He was aware of her deep blue eyes and steady gaze. She had a faint fragrance of tropical flowers. There was no way this vision of beauty could offend him.

Ward touched her shoulder, "That is kind of you to ask." He removed his touch and answered, "I simply don't see the point in alcohol. I want every wit I have available. I also don't know why a six dollar drink would quench my thirst more than a one dollar coke. By the end of the month that's forty or fifty dollars I can save or spend elsewhere. There is no recovery program just practical sense on my part. Would you prefer I order something else?"

"Oh no, no, no," she replied with a warm smile. "I really agree with you, but I have fallen in with the wine crowd. Just think, if we both followed your plan we would have a hundred dollars or more to save or spend elsewhere. Like a supper out." He thought her eyes became even more sparkly, and she might be making a social suggestion.

"But the professional question I have," Becky continued, "is about your home visits. My office was told by a family that you came to their home to see if there was something that could help their daughter's math performance. Is that correct? Do you visit all your students?"

"Wow, I hope they weren't offended or complaining. I visited just two families whose students are falling behind the class. In both cases they have conflicting obligations that keep them from their homework exercise. I hoped I could advocate either a later bedtime, which is a poor fix, or a rest from church attendance for one and volleyball for the other. If they can improve their scores they can still pass the class." Ward looked at his folded hands on the table. "I'm, vain enough to believe that I can get every student through this successfully. No one left behind."

Becky placed her hand on top of his and he noticed a tear forming in her eyes.

"Am I in trouble with the district?" Ward murmured. "I didn't see a problem in a home visit." She shook her head and patted his hand, which encouraged him to say, "I've come to believe that being kind is superior to being correct."

She removed her hand and said, "My dissertation mentor used to say that very same thing. Ward, you really are a special teacher now. I'm curious to know what has caused the marvelous turnaround from a teacher with two unfavorable evaluations and probation to one that receives such praise from your students." That she was aware of his Spokane failure was news to Ward. That the students grade their teacher was also news.

"I don't know," he said with a shake of his head. "I was angry, confused, and bitter as can be when I went to Spokane. I'm sure a lot of fear was mixed into that. The deceit and callus brutality of the beating did something very dark to my soul. I think the year of probation was a time when I began to let that go and became more aware of all the good around me rather than the bad that had overwhelmed me. I noticed the great people I work with and how delightful these students can be. I'll also tell you that the past two weeks has been wonderful meeting you."

"I agree," she said with a warm smile. "Who knew that Giggles could be more than a routine evening out with friends?"

Thinking back to her innuendo about a meal together he took a deep breath and asked, "I have a pending Sunday brunch with parents of one of my students. She has encouraged me to bring a plus one. Would you consider attending with me? They were here for my one and only stand-up and I think they are involved with Republican politics. She hasn't set a date yet, but we agreed it would be before the holidays." That was a very lengthy and leggy invitation. They were both wondering if he was nervous about it.

Another open mic stand-up was getting started so Becky answered, "Ward, may we step out into the lobby where we won't distract others?" She was standing as she said it. Moments later they were alone and she said, "This is a wonderful evening. It is light and full of promise I think. I feel safe and free enough with you that I can be honest. Your stand-up showed me that you are focused and steadfast. You don't seem to be distracted by the inane. I liked that a lot." Then taking a deep breath, she added, "When you asked about attending a Sunday brunch with other couples, I flinched. I haven't been on any sort of a date for a long time, even a gentle social gathering." She reached for his hand and gently held it. "Even what may seem like a little date is major to me. You don't know it but you are also helping me bloom again.

I was married nine years ago. We met our sophomore year and married after graduation. I became pregnant a year later. Jess went into the army just after our daughter was born. In his second deployment to Iraq he was killed by a roadside bomb. That is the source of the tears when you said, 'No one left behind.'" She took a deep breath and continued, "Even though it's been seven years, this evening is the first time I have welcomed an invitation to socialize with another man." The words were spoken softly but the impact of their meaning was deliberate.

Before she could say anything more, Ward interrupted, "What did you name your daughter?" His expression was warm and relaxed and she knew he had asked the proper question at the proper time. "We named her Sophia, which means," Ward's voice joined hers as they said together, "Wisdom."

"I love the name Sophie," he said with a smile. "It sounds happy and fun while having a twist of sophisticated smarts to boot."

She started to release his hand, but he held on to hers. "Ward, I have a lot of baggage and an eight year old little girl. I wanted to tell you this so you would not be embarrassed by asking a complicated older woman to brunch."

With a sincere smile he said, "Now that's funny. There is no remote possibility you could be an embarrassment to me. It sounds like we both have heavy things from the past that we have overcome." Changing his expression to a puzzled scowl, he added, "And what is this older stuff about?"

"Well I just turned thirty two and you are just getting started." She was grateful he had not released her hand.

"Well I'm just getting started at Roosevelt, but I'm thirty two as well," he said in a playful tone of voice. "When is your birthday?"

"I just celebrated October second," she said proudly.

"Ha! Mine is September thirtieth," he said in a voice loud enough that some inside could have heard him. Then in a more proper voice he added, "I'm two days older than you! I'll bet we were both conceived as a New Year celebration." His expression returned to gentle caring. "Now that we have that out of the way, how about a brunch date? It would be pretty safe in the daylight with six other adults."

"May I think about it a couple days. Maybe you could give me a call with the details." She wasn't feeling rushed by Ward; she was restricted by her own anxiety.

"Of course I would love a reason to call you, but before you parachute away, remember that we are only talking about a brunch, a late breakfast. It's not like we're buying a car together or taking out a second mortgage. I really hope you will want to do this." He released her hand and they returned to table sixteen just as the open mic was over.

The second week of November was an important time. It was time to select the algebra grades. To be fair about it, Ward distributed folded cards upon which he had written a number and a grade. "For clarity," he explained, "and for your privacy, there are no names, and I promise that I did not use an alphabetical process. Look at the grade on your card then think about how you have done on the exercises to number them. Maybe the card is higher, and maybe it is not. You get to choose your grade. If you are happy with the grade on the card, just draw a star on it and hand it back to me. If you want the aggregate score from your exercises, draw a circle around the grade on the card and place a diagonal line through it. I'll understand what that means."

When he tallied the grades seventeen of them chose the aggregate and agreed to delete the initial grade Ward had written. "Wow, he thought, "seventeen out of twenty two is about 80% improvement. Four of the five that had changed their grade had opted for the initial grade; one which was better than their recollection of the exercises. Only Ginger Jameson had selected the initial grade on the card which was less than her perfect performance on the exercises.

It was also an important time because Becky had agreed to attend the brunch with Ward. He was grateful for the three lengthy evening phone calls that had given him a deeper insight to her hesitance and an opportunity to quiet her anxieties and assure her of his sincere desire to have an opportunity to get to know her. He learned that she had lived with her mom since Jess's death. At first she was in deep grief and her mom was a tremendous help in caring for Sophie. Finally getting her doctorate was a shift in focus and a positive challenge that stabilized her world. On top of that crucial information, he learned that her mom was also a widow because Terrance Stanley, Becky's dad, was one of the four firefighters killed in the Pang Warehouse fire, when she was nineteen years old. Becky's life had known great grief twice. No wonder she was hesitant to go on a date with anyone other than her table sixteen friends. That understanding caused Ward to admire her even more and want to protect her from further pain.

BRUNCH

He found Lakemont Drive inside the Sand Point Golf Course. Becky helped him find the correct address of the impressive home that looked out at Lake Washington and further east to the Cascades, which had a fresh powdering of snow. Even on this cloudy day it was beautiful.

"Oh my," she said softly. "This is a marvelous vista. I wonder if they ever get tired of looking at it."

As Ward rang the doorbell he answered in that same soft voice, "I'm thinking there are some things that are so lovely they are always mesmerizing." She turned to look into his innocent smile understanding his intended compliment.

Peggy opened the door. "I'm glad you could find us up here on the ridge," she said welcoming them in.

Bob joined her and immediately began laughing to Ward's surprise. Becky began to laugh along with him. "It is a delightfully small world," Bob finally got out. "Welcome to our home Miss Rhodes." The puzzle stopped Ward halfway over the threshold.

Becky turned to inform Ward, "Doctor Robert was my dissertation mentor. He is chairman of the Graduate Psychology Department of UW. I had no idea we were coming to his home." She turned to offer her hand to Peggy, saying, "It is wonderful to meet you, ma'am." Ward joined in the greeting handshakes.

As they walked into the elegant living room with panoramic windows looking out at the mountain vista, Peggy said, "I'd like you to meet our friends Jim and Sally Peterson. While handshakes were being exchanged, she went on, "He's our Congressman for the fifth district and she is an attorney in the Prosecuting Attorney's Office." Turning to the other couple, she said, "And these are our friends Sam and Nancy Whitward. He's on the staff of the Treasurer, and she is Information Director for the Governor. Please be gentle with these folks. With a Democrat taking over the Whitehouse we have all had a trying summer." Handshakes and smiles were unanimous.

Ginger came out of the kitchen to greet the new guests. With a shy smile she shook Becky's hand saying, "Any friend of Mr. Winter is a friend of mine. I'm delighted to meet you Miss Rhodes." It was a very memorable beginning to brunch.

When the marvelous meal was finished, their host came around once more with a bottle of champagne and a pitcher of orange juice. "May I refresh your Mimosa?" he asked.

Ward slid his glass and answered, "I would love a bit more juice, but I'll pass on the champagne."

Becky pushed her glass near his and added, "As will I. We are on an austerity plan saving up for a dinner out at the end of the month." Her gracious smile was meant more for Ward than their host.

Nancy asked, "Ward, Peggy tells me you have a fresh teaching system. Can you tell us a bit about that?"

"Well I'm not sure how fresh it is because I am using the same textbook all the other classes have used. Perhaps we just have a bit more fun at it," he answered.

She asked again, "But you are teaching algebra aren't you? How can that be fun?"

Ward noticed a smile blossom on both Peggy and Ginger's face. "I depend on our textbook of course," he answered. "But like any tool, there are a variety of ways it can be used. I believe every one of my students wants to complete the requirement, so it is my job to help him or her do that. I try to be courteous as well as playful. I try to treat them as they wish all teachers would." He realized how opposite that declaration was from his attitude in Spokane.

"That sounds delightful," Sally joined the conversation. "But how effective can that relaxed attitude be? How many of your students are getting it?" Her face seemed concerned rather than supportive.

"Well, I have 71 algebra students in three classes who are all passing with a C or better grade. In the trigonometry class there are nineteen students. Only two of them are at risk, and I think we can still recover a passing grade for them."

The congressman asked in a surprised voice, "You are telling us that out of ninety students only two have a less than C average grade, and they may still improve? How can you accomplish that?"

Ward smiled in a relaxed way and asked, "Do you play golf, sir?" When Mr. Peterson nodded, Ward continued, "Do you play with friends who allow you to take a mulligan on the first tee?" The congressman nodded with a wider smile. "I gave a one time oops on the first couple days. It demonstrated that I was an ally and that accuracy was mandatory. Then he looked at Ginger. "I don't want to put you on the spot," he said to his student. "I can give him the formal answer or you can tell him how much fun we are having."

"He is telling you the truth'" the smiling young lady said quietly. "Algebra is my favorite class. As soon as I get home I do my homework. It only takes a few minutes and I double check to make sure that it is correct so I will get a tootsie roll. I don't like math, but Mr. Winter makes it feel more like a party. I don't want this year to be over." Her gracious smile was a testament to the teacher.

Peggy added, "He tosses a tootsie roll to each student who has a correct exercise."

"Really?" Jim grinned. "Can you explain how that makes any difference?" The congressman was engaged in the discussion.

Ward was confident that no rules had been violated so he was relaxed as he explained, "Yes sir, I believe the difference is in the reward attitude. In a regular twelve week quarter an abstract reward is at the end. That is a delayed grade, which is scarcely connected to the work that it represents. On the other hand, a tidbit of candy is an immediate and playful reward. It builds an achieving community as each student demonstrates satisfaction. It represents an instant and concrete grade. I was sure to ask if there were any allergies or diabetics in the class first."

Jim nodded and asked another question. "Did you learn that in graduate school? None of my teachers were dialed into that notion." He paused again, then asked, "And I hear you also do stand-up comedy. Does that help with your classroom task?"

Ward looked at Peggy and said in an alarmed voice, "I thought we agreed to keep that a buried secret." Then looking at Jim he said, "I think the initial idea of tootsie rolls came out of a faculty meeting when we were trying to imagine what might help us connect with our students. I wish I had connected better with the Giggles crowd. I felt like I shanked that one. I called my foster father after the lamentable first and only effort. He blamed the M. C. for asking a mathematician to solve a problem. I guess I am just a one note samba."

"I don't know what that means," the congressman said. "But I do know that two of my friends who were in the Giggles crowd were so positively impressed they urged us to come and meet someone who is willing to see the problems in our system and speak up about it. I like your style Ward and personally I hope that was not your only moment to speak out. Our country has been blessed by intelligent men and women who have spoken out."

With a grin, Ward said softly, "I think there is a lot that is very right about our country. But obviously there are some gigantic problems and I think we cannot solve those problems by ignoring them."

Becky chuckled, "That's the second time you have quoted my mentor. What's going on with you guys?" She looked at Ward and then Dr. Jameson.

Perhaps their host understood Ward's desire to change the subject because he said to Becky, "Brilliance knows no boundaries. Speaking of achievement, I understand your dissertation has gone to a publisher to be circulated around the country. "'Testing Children of Trauma' is going to serve a host of little folks who have not been understood. Becky you must be very proud of your accomplishment too. You two are a winning couple." Both she and Ward blushed, embarrassed by the attention.

The conversation shifted to the news from Olympia and the challenges for the Republican minority. There were several important proposals that were dying in committee for lack of support, and a young group of activists that called themselves the Tea Party were drawing attention. They had plans for the next election. They had hope that they could reestablish influence for a conservative change. Finally just before two o'clock, Peggy made sure that Ward and Becky were invited to the first quarter meeting of the caucus. "We meet in the downtown Sheraton. The January eighth meeting will be a dinner meeting with several speakers planned. Bob and I would be delighted if you would be our guests. The hosted bar is open at 6 and the invocation is promptly at 7. I'll call you for a confirmation a couple days before. I really hope you can be there. You would add a lot to the caucus."

On the way home they both had observations to share. Becky said, "I had no idea we would see Dr. Jameson, or get to meet his family and such distinguished friends. I really liked talking with them."

The car was quiet until Ward said, "I really like talking with you. I haven't had this much fun ever with someone else."

"I feel very comfortable with you as well. It feels like I'm always smiling when we talk together," Becky said with a warm look at him. She paused for a moment, then asked, "Ward, are you comfortable enough with me to tell me about your past? I heard you mention your foster dad. I'd like to hear about that. And I haven't heard anything about former love interests. Are you currently involved with anyone? I'd like to hear about that too, if you don't feel like I am prying."

A hint of a smile stayed on Ward's face and his voice was very soft. "I am very comfortable with you. I think it is because you are so affirming and not demanding or judgmental." After another pause, he added, "There is nothing interesting about my past. In the birth order I am number three, with an older brother, Michael, and a sister, Chrissy. My parents divorced when I was a first grader. Michael went with dad. My mom was so irresponsible she lost custody of me when I was in middle school and Chrissy was either in Juvenile Detention or rehab. For three years I was bouncing around different foster homes. I felt angry most of the time because I was afraid my world was going to completely fall apart. I had lost just about everything. Then the Harts made me feel safe and loved. When I could finally trust that, it was the door of opportunity."

He chuckled the way you do when there is nothing humorous. "As for ladies in my life, I've never had a romantic relationship with a woman, or been kissed." Becky gave him a sad grimace. "A moment of interest was the one in Ellensburg that baited me into a mugging, which tore two years out of my life. The beating left emotional wounds that were very difficult for me and lasting reminders. I have this large scar on my head and steel plates on my skull and hip. That may be why I'm uncomfortable around most women. You have been a wonderful exception. I feel like I am just now, with you, leaving that sad account behind me."

She gave a tiny chuckle before saying, "We're quite a pair. You have ghosts in your past with hardware but no baggage and I have ghosts plus some sweet baggage. Do you think that is why we gravitated toward one another?"

"I know I should agree with you, Becky. I've been wondering if you and I are children of trauma, as you have identified them. Perhaps that is our similarity. But to be super honest, like a guy I think I was drawn to your beautiful blue eyes, the fragrance of flowers and your warm touch. It's like we are old friends. I think you are a lovely woman and I'm a lucky fellow to be in this conversation with you. She placed her hand on his arm with a shy smile. For a couple minutes nothing was said. Finally Ward broke the silence saying, "How would you like to stop somewhere for a cup of coffee, or does that sound goofy?"

"Want to hear something funny?" Becky asked. "I was just wondering if I could invite you in for a cup of coffee to introduce you to mom and Sophie. Is it too soon for that, or is that goofy?" Her smile added a playful bit of a squint.

"It is never too soon to do the right thing," he answered. "I would love to meet your mom and the only young lady I know named Sophie." He nodded his agreement.

"Ward, in some very tender way you remind me of how I miss my granddad. He often spoke those one line truisms that seem to come naturally from you too. They are easy to remember. He once said, 'Everyone needs a friend to be goofy with.' You prove his point. Here we are stuffed full as ticks trying to think of ways to stretch our afternoon together just a bit with a cup of coffee."

With a chuckle, Ward repeated, "Someone to be goofy with. I so love that idea. May I use that in my inventory? I think it explains what I have always wanted but never had, someone to be goofy with." He chuckled a bit happier.

SOPHIE

After a gracious introduction, Sophie even wanted to show Ward her kitty Silvia, so everyone would know everyone. Becky had trouble controlling her tears, she was so happy. "We've had Silvia for a long time," she chuckled, trying to control her emotions. "She's an old girl now. She was a tiny kitten that was just dumped in the street when I scooped her out of a busy Aurora Avenue."

Ward had a distant flashback to an afternoon when he could have been right behind that rescue. He chose not to say anything more about it. Instead, he explained that his home on Winona Avenue was only about five minutes away on Aurora. Before he had moved in he had the kitchen and master bathroom remodeled, but the old house still had a long list of remodel needs. "The front yard is small on a triangular lot, and the backyard is huge. I haven't decided what to do with that." He explained that his foster folks had a beautiful home on Phinney Ave. "Steve is the manager of a downtown Toyota dealership." There was tons of information to exchange, and a thought to consider, the incredible possibility that their paths may have crossed fourteen years ago.

Lois served a platter of grilled cheese sandwiches and fruit punch. They watched America's Funniest Home Videos and everyone agreed with Sophie that the kitties were the cutest. When it was time to go Ward tried to express his gratitude to them all for a most memorable afternoon. He promised to stay in touch. All the way home he thought about blue, blue eyes and the fragrance of tropical flowers.

When he shared with Nora how pleasant his weekend had been, she wondered if she might invite them to a Thanksgiving dinner. It would be a real treat to have a few more at the table. Ward agreed that he would be very much in favor of that idea, but would leave the details to her. It turned out to be a spectacular feast. Afterward both Nora and Steve agreed that Becky was a delightful lady with wit and charm. And most of all they enjoyed Sophie who seemed to have many entertaining stories to share.

"Hi, it's me," her voice was warm and welcome. "I hope this isn't too late to call. I know we were with your folks just yesterday, but I feel like we missed Giggles last night and I miss you tonight."

"Hi lovely lady, I'm glad to hear your voice too. It was really fun being together at the folks' yesterday." Ward wondered if this was just a chat or if there was a reason for Becky's call.

"We were just getting the Thank You cards written before Sophie went to bed. She asked me to call you especially to thank you for the book. She said she would read a story from 'My Kitty' to Silvia every night. That was very thoughtful of you." There was almost a snicker in her voice. "I waited as long as I could before picking up the phone. It feels wonderful to have a friend to chat with." That made her voice soften and get a bit breathy.

"Have we found a friend to goof around with?" he asked in the same soft way.

"I think we have," she replied, and then added, "I really hope we have." They chatted for nearly an hour. The only reason for the call was personal enjoyment. He found a reason to call her on Saturday evening, and she called him Sunday evening.

They had chatted for a few minutes before she opened a serious subject. "Sophie wants me to invite you to her caroling program at the church. I have the impression that you may not be inclined to attend. May we talk a bit about that? Am I correct in thinking you would rather talk about a root canal than church?" Her voice had the lightness that charmed him always.

Ward was quiet for just a moment then replied, "I've never had a root canal. But my only brush with religion was in foster homes that ended with me running for safety from fanatics. There was a foster home run by extreme Christians who tried to bully me to join with them. I have had an aversion to it ever since then, but it was never given any adult consideration. The Harts might attend occasionally, but it was never discussed there either."

He was quiet for so long she asked, "Does that mean you would rather not discuss it with me... now?"

"No, it means I don't know where to start. You must know that I care for you enough to discuss anything. So the short answer is, if Sophie would like me to attend, I will gladly be there. Where and when is the only information I need."

Becky's voice became as soft as a whisper. "Thank you. That sort of shows me your open and generous spirit. I have always felt that if your life is not all you want it to be, it may be that you have some forgiving to do. Let me tell you my story. That might be a place to begin. When my dad died in that fire, I was just getting ready for the UW. Mom and I were in terrible shock. We could not understand how such a perfect man could be taken from us. We blamed Pang, the fire department, his team mates, just about anyone we could think about, even God. It was only through the gentle care of the church and the comfort of faith that got us through it. That vacancy in my heart might have also been motivation for me to marry Jess. But then just three years later when he was killed I was overwhelmed with grief all over again. If it wasn't for my awareness of a loving God who was beside me, gently comforting, strengthening and encouraging me to continue, I don't know what I would have done." She was quiet for a moment and then added, "I believe there is a huge difference between religion, which is so often wrestling with some creed system, and a loving awareness that we have a personal relationship with the Lord and are never alone. God is always with us. That's what Sophie wants to sing about, baby Jesus in a manger, God with us." There was a thoughtful silence as both were thinking about her statement.

"I want what she's having," Ward said with a sigh. "What could be more wonderful than the wisdom of Wisdom?" They shared a relaxed chuckle but knew that they were not in the same place they had been in just a few moments ago.

"Thank you, my sweet friend" he said sincerely. I feel like we just shared a tender hug. I have a ton of things to think about now."

"I'll tell Sophie that you wrote it on your calendar: Green Lake Presbyterian Church December 11th at 7 o'clock." They chatted for another few minutes. He called her on Monday evening and she called him Tuesday evening. When they were together at Giggles, he offered to bring pizza over for Friday evening. He was sure her granddad was correct. "Everybody needs a friend to be goofy with." She called him on Saturday evening and he called her on Sunday.

CALLED TO THE DISTRICT OFFICE

Monday afternoon when the intercom in the faculty room informed him he had a call, Ward smiled believing he knew who it might be. To his surprise it was the receptionist at the Seattle District office.

"Mr. Winter, your grade report is being reviewed by Dr. Stanton the comptroller tomorrow afternoon at 4 o'clock. He invites you to bring whatever substantiating documentation you might have to clear up his confusion." Suddenly ghosts from Spokane Valley and the nauseating aroma of failure shuddered back to life. He shook his head denying them to blunt the new attitude he was forging.

The next afternoon he borrowed the custodian's hand truck and loaded four boxes into his car. When he arrived at the 3rd Avenue S district offices of the Seattle Schools he received curious glances but since he was not delivering items for anyone, he was allowed to wait until Dr. Stanton was ready for him.

"Good afternoon Mr. Winter. What is all this?" the congenial man asked.

"I was told to bring substantiating documentation for my grade report. I hope there is no problem." Ward worked to calm his jitters and appear relaxed.

"I'll tell you the truth, Ward." He was glad to hear his first name used instead of a formal one. "When I saw that unbelievable list of grades, I recalled that you are the same man who had two unfavorable evaluations and were on probation last year. Can you see why I am somewhat confused? You have given 90 students at least a passing grade and most received an A grade."

"It is surprising to me as well, sir. But if you will look a couple years further back you will see the disabling attack I received at Central and the long recovery process. I'm really not the same teacher I was at Harris High School." Ward seemed relaxed and focused. "I have surrounded myself with excellent colleagues and supportive friends. I have accepted a fresh confidence that has found a new positive response from the students."

"I'm glad for your recovery," the controller said softly. "That must have been a very difficult time. But Mr. Winter, you are asking me to believe that each and every one of your students did passing work in mathematics. That is difficult for me and the other staff here to believe." Nodding toward the four boxes, he continued, "I'm very curious what might be in the boxes."

"I was instructed to bring substantiating material, sir. Each box contains the work a class has done. There is a manila folder for each student. In that folder you will find 44 daily quizzes that we called exercises. There is also a midterm and final exam which we called 'round-up'. I know that it is excessive, but it is the material I used to establish each grade."

With a warm smile Dr. Stanton said, "You were anxious about a grilling weren't you? You brought the whole kitchen sink to demonstrate the truth. The auditor in me appreciates thoroughness and the teacher in me recognizes quality when it is in front of me. We have spent all of ten minutes together and I can tell how you are bringing a fresh style of education to Roosevelt. Thank you, Ward. We are soon going into the Holiday,… I wish we could still call it Christmas,… break. May I keep these until school resumes in January?"

"Yes, sir, they were headed for the basement storage anyway. Please keep them as long as you like. By the way, is Dr. Rhode's office in this building? If she hasn't already left, I'd like to say hello. She is one of the excellent support people who have made the pleasant change in me."

CAROLING A NEW SONG

The church parking lot had plenty of open spaces. Ward chose one near the street light with easy access and visibility. Caution had become his habit. Inside there was much to see as he followed the arrows to the sanctuary. It felt strange to him and at the same time welcoming. A smiling lady greeted him and offered a page of carols and readings. He noticed Lois sitting near the side aisle and asked if he could join her. She scooted over a ways and invited him into the pew. Quietly she informed him, "Becca is back helping the kids get ready. She'll join us in just a few minutes." His eyes were drinking in the graceful banners and seasonal symbols.

Lois moved a bit closer so she could quietly say, "Your mom invited us over for a New Year's Eve dinner." That was the first time Ward had heard about the plan. "I told her we would be happy to come, if you folks would come to our house for a Christmas Eve dinner. Do you think that would be too much of a good thing?"

Ward whispered his reply, "So far we are enjoying one another a lot. Isn't it better to try and see, rather than not try and regret it later?" They both grinned as she patted his knee. Becky joined them just as the lights were dimmed. She sat on the other side of Ward.

A light illuminated the reader who read about angels announcing the birth of Jesus and the organ began the familiar tune of *"Angels We Have Heard on High"*. With the singing of the second verse a group of children, including Sophie, entered dressed as angels with flowing white robes and haloes. The stage lights brightened and the curtain opened to reveal the familiar nativity scene with Mary and Joseph kneeling beside a cradle. After a scripture reading, the organ played *"The First Noel."* Ward had a large smile when he realized he was between two very lovely voices. A group of children entered from the back of the stage to sing *"The Friendly Beasts."* Each class had a verse and was sort of dressed to represent the animals in the stable. They increased their volume when it came to sheep with a curly horn and shepherds with crooks walked down the aisle to gather around the nativity scene. The congregation was invited to sing *"Away in a Manger.* There was another reading about the three wise men; it was made more memorable with a bit of an error. The lad read that the visitors brought gold, frankincense, and mirth. The congregation chuckled at the changed word. With the singing of the first and last verses of the carol three boys wearing bathrobes and Burger King crowns brought their offerings to the nativity gathering. A pastor prayed a gentle prayer of gratitude. Then after thanking the participants, she invited the congregation to stand and with mirth, sing *"Joy to the World."*

Ward was surprised at his response to the brief program. Actually he was amazed at the light, joyful curiosity it brought him. Perhaps the immaturity of the children spoke to his own level of understanding, or lack thereof. The positive innocence of the program was a direct contradiction of what he had experienced before as religion. He was pretty sure that he would be reading the scripture account and talking with a certain lady about it.

Becky said quietly, "Sophie expects us to stop at Dairy Queen on the way home for a chocolate sundae as tribute to the evening. It is sort of a tradition with us. Would you like to join us?" Her gracious smile and charm were becoming very important to Ward.

"I'd love too," he replied, "if you will let me pay. I feel like I have not been doing my share."

"As you wish, sir," she said with a warm smile. "I think the important thing to Sophie is that you are with us. I think she has a crush on you." There was a heart beat before she added softly, "And I think I do too."

Ward reached for her hand, interlocking their fingers together. "Me too," he said as softly, "with both of you. Who knew a caroling program could be this much fun?"

Later at home, Ward was browsing his computer looking for New Year's cards. He found many elegant business cards which were much too formal, and then he found one that was perfect. With only a little customizing he ordered a hundred cards that said "Happy" at the top, and "New Year" at the bottom. In between was a picture of a Tootsie Roll! Inside he had printed, "We can have a Tootsie New Year! Best wishes, Ward Winter." He had never felt like it was his obligation to send wishes to his students, but this seemed like a most unusual year. Instead of an obligation, he felt it was a privilege.

It was the last Thursday night before the winter break. Ward and Becky arrived early believing they would reserve table sixteen. To their surprise, Jay and Florence were already there and they were holding hands.

Jay said with a bright smile. "We were just talking about you two. Do you have any plans for the break? We would like to go to the Fisherman's Grill on pier seventy and wondered if you would join us." They continued to hold hands.

Becky answered before Ward, "That sounds fun. Sophie visits her grandparents in Gig Harbor for four days. If it could be one of those, I think we would be free." She looked at Ward for verification. That was the first Ward had heard about extended family and Sophie's absence. "Let's look at our calendars when we get home. I'll call you," she said looking at Florence

Florence looked toward the door and added, "We hoped it could just be the four of us. I'm very grateful how this fall has turned out." She gave Jay a happy smile. "I think Lou is going to call table sixteen tonight. The topic is dating and he thinks he's cute by putting me on the spot." She waited a moment for any comment. When there was none she added, "He would have been my brother-in-law, if Roger had been a more honest person. I'll tell you about it later." She saw Sam and Maria enter; they were also holding hands. Florence's smile grew even larger.

Two other tables were called before Lou, the M.C., called out, "Let's hear from…. table sixteen!" As Florence stood, he chuckled, "Hey, it's our friend Florence from Puyallup." He handed her the mike saying more warmly, "The subject is dating and the floor is all yours." The insinuating smile was only enjoyable to him.

"Howdy y'all," she said in a rich drawl accent. "You're lookin' mighty fine tonight. I'm supposed to talk about datin', but hell, more than half of y'all are doing that right now. The other half is doin' somethin' else under the table. It's like I'm preachin' to the choir." There was a playful ripple of laughter.

"Lordy, Lordy, when I think on it I do believe datin' is a lot like car shoppin'; you know what I mean? First you make a list of what kind of car you might be interested in. You know, it's got to be dependable, affordable, comfortable, safe and good lookin'. Aren't those pretty much what you look for in a date ladies?" The audience gave another ripple of appreciation. "On top of that he has got to be someone you are not ashamed to be with, you know, doesn't drinks too much, flirt with other girls in front of you, talk too loud or chew with his mouth open. Well that last one is optional if you do too." The laughter was a bit louder. "I'm just sayin' that you make a list of what you're lookin' for."

She shook her head and said in a disappointed voice, "Then you go to talk to a car salesman. Lordy, Lordy they tell stories. They'll tell you its brand spankin' new when they have rolled the odometer back a hundred thousand. It's like talkin' to a married man who just wants a warm bed for the night. He'll tell you just what you want to hear to get you to go out with him. Lordy, Lordy! I told a salesman I wanted a white car. He said he had a perfect blue one that just matched my eyes. Crap, if I wanted to match my eyes I would've asked him for a bloodshot red one. I had a tough one last night!" After understanding laughter, she went on. "They just say anythin' to make a sale. How much of a sell job did the guy you're with give you?" There was more laughter from the ladies in the house.

"Like I said, it's like buyin' a car. You make a list and then you go to one car lot after another. Do you pay any attention to your list? Hell no! You listen to your heart that tells you this is the most wonderful car you've ever been able to own! It has leather bucket seats and a sound system better'n yours at home. It's shiny new and smells delicious. For men it's a lot more complicated. Some of them want a truck with great... big...," she held her cupped hands in front of her breasts and several men cheered, "tires, so they can play in the dirt and mud." There was more laughter in response to her double meaning. "For others its huge engine has got to make more noise than Dale Earnhardt's. Some want a four wheeler that can take them huntin' into the mountains and others want an SUV with a fold-out Murphy bed, and you can bet it's not ducks they're after." More laughter and applause filled the room.

"Ooops, there goes my yellow light. Like I said, datin' is like buyin' a car. I had my list all thought out, but when that cowboy took me by the hand and guided me to the dance floor, he pulled me tight against that hard... belt buckle. My knees went weak and I knew this was the one for me, list or not. In my opinion you'll never find the right one until you stop lookin' for him or her.... and just listen to your heart."

Her light went red and she waved and thanked the folks for listening, amid spirited applause. Those seated at tables fifteen and sixteen cheered with pure appreciation.

Two more tables were called to complete the hour. It was time to go, or pay a cover charge for the table when true stand-up comedians were scheduled. Ward announced that his home was about five minutes away. "If you would like to see a bachelor cave, I have a box of doughnuts and plenty of liquid refreshments. Here's my address or you can just follow me. There is usually plenty of parking on Winona." He offered folks a piece of paper.

Jay and Florence said they would love to see Ward's home and Sam and Maria agreed they would join them, but only for a few minutes. It was still a school night.

Ten minutes later, the group was exploring the sparsely filled house. Only a cursory peek revealed a cavernous basement which held both challenge and promise of useable space. Upstairs was much the same with five small bedrooms, a bathroom and a sitting room. The main floor, where they enjoyed the doughnuts and hot chocolate, had a large living room and dining room separated only by an attractive arch. The kitchen was not large, but had obviously received some recent modernizing. A bathroom, den and main bedroom completed the tour. Each person had different thoughts about Ward's home.

Florence thought, "With just a little fixing, there could be enough rental space for four or five of my friends to share expenses and have a very affordable community."

Jay thought, "This place could easily be a gem! This is large enough for a big family and located only minutes from downtown, with a lake to hike around!"

Sam thought, "Only Ward would come up with this incredible house. The basement is big enough for a giant media room with a pool table and mini-bar."

Maria thought, "How will he ever afford to put new furniture in here? Who will clean this? It looks like a fulltime job for a housekeeper."

Becky thought, "He never ceases to amaze me. I can only imagine what his creativity will do with this, but I'll bet it will be fabulous! I just hope I get to see it happen"

Ward thought, "I'll bet they either think I'm completely deranged or simply ignorant."

Before everyone left, Jay asked Ward, "Would you mind if my brother contacts you? His name is Phillip; he's with a company called Reno Masters in Bellingham. They have a series on the Home and Garden channel. You did say that you own this free and clear, didn't you? If you can get a home improvement loan, he can make your dollars go twice as far. It really is remarkable and this is the finest candidate for their genius I've ever seen."

While Ward and Becky cleaned up the hot chocolate cups they chatted about Florence's stand-up. "Her southern drawl was really entertaining," he reflected. "I thought she was both believable and wise."

Becky had a serious expression as she answered, "She was into drama at Western. That's where she and Roger got together. He was a charming finance major, who seemed bound for success. They were living together after she got her Bachelor's degree. Then when he was discovered embezzling from a doctor's clinic instead of managing their money, he spent three or four years in prison. Because they were sharing a bank account, she lost all her savings in the settlement. It was heartbreaking for her." Becky looked at him in that tender way that made him want to hug her. "I think everyone gets a portion of grief in their life. Florence went back to school to get her doctorate in admin with some help from her family. That's where she first saw Jay. He was working on his Master's and they never really met. I think that's why she came to your table after your stand-up. She recognized him." Becky placed her hand on Ward's arm. "Wait, I didn't mean you were just an excuse for her." Her eyes were searching his. "I'm sure she really meant every word she said that night. You were the reason she came to your table." She stepped closer to him. "I'm rambling because I really want to..." She moved a tiny bit closer and kissed him gently. His arms embraced her and she hugged him for an extended moment.

"Oh my!" she whispered. "Ward, forgive me if that was impertinent of me, or out of line." She took a deep breath and finished, "I've been planning for that to be a Christmas Eve surprise. I remember you mentioned that you have never been kissed. I've wanted to do that since the caroling program. I'm so glad you allowed me to be the first." She snickered a tiny bit while he continued to hold her. "Perhaps I could repeat the gift then."

As he released his embrace, Ward said softly. "I think I do believe in Santa Claus now and there is no need for an apology. I'm grateful she came to our table for whatever reason because ultimately it has led to this moment. You are wonderful." They both chuckled to relieve some delightful energy.

As Ward was driving Becky home, she explained that tomorrow evening was the last opportunity to take Sophie shopping for a couple of last minute gifts, and of course the secret Santa gifts. Her mom had sent a card to each of them with the name of the person for whom they could provide a Christmas Eve gift. It would be a pleasant way to get ready for Christmas morning.

CHRISTMAS EVE DINNER

In fact, it was far more than pleasant. Ward gazed at these five other folks at the table who had become the most cherished part of his life. He reflected that a year ago the three of them had opened gifts and while they were generous, they lacked the glitter of wonder and the magic of affection. He was certain that Sophie didn't deserve all the credit, but she was the candidate for the most excited, and the most joyous. It was a marvelous contagious part of the evening, complete with a sprig of mistletoe that was used more than once. Nora gave Steve a leather bound calendar with all the important dates of next year she wanted him to remember; Steve gave Lois a soft lap robe for watching television; Lois gave Becky a frilly seasonal apron and dish towels for the kitchen; Becky gave Sophie a color by number book with a set of colored pencils; Sophie happily gave Ward a bag of Tootsie Rolls; and Ward gave Nora a pair of warm slippers for cozy lounging. It was a delightful evening for each one.

As it was drawing to a close, Ward smiled as he asked himself, "If it's this good this year, what will next year be like?" He spent Christmas morning with Steve and Nora and the afternoon with Lois, Becky and Sophie. The Rhodes from Gig Harbor picked Sophie up for their annual visit.

On Monday Nora gave Lois an important phone call. "Hi Lois, yes it was a most enjoyable evening. They are looking more like a family, I agree. Listen the reason I am calling is to tell you about a special part of our New Year's Eve dinner. For the past four years we have included a man from Steve's office. His name is Nick Morris; he's the finance man for the dealership. His wife died after a very long battle with cancer. His son is an officer in the navy on a submarine somewhere secret and his daughter is a missionary doctor in Puerto Rico. We've sort of become his fill-in family. I didn't think he would intrude on our plans. Would you mind if he joins us?"

"Nora," she answered almost immediately, "you are so thoughtful to warn me. I do not mind a bit. In fact it would be pleasant to chat with a new friend. I heard Ward recently say that if we don't risk anything, we risk even more. He has certainly brought a wonderful new element to our family. You must be very proud of him."

"We are indeed. He is regularly telling us how grateful he is to be part of our family. We have tried to express our gratitude for what he has brought to us."

Lois asked, "Do I understand that he is a foster son?"

"Yes, he came to us just before he started high school. He had been shuffled around a lot and we were happy to offer him some stability." They chatted for several minutes without mentioning the reason for Nora's call again. Apparently Lois had no misgivings about one more at the table.

Becky called Ward later that evening and he called her on Tuesday. Before their chat was finished, she asked him about his Wednesday plans. "You do remember that we are going to meet Florence and Jay at 6:30 don't you? He assured her that was on his agenda, but then he admitted that he was pretty much rattling around the old house trying to imagine what he could do with it. She asked if she could pick up some burgers and join him. "I'm not sure what I can offer, but at least I could take notes. I think that between us we have some pretty creative ideas." It was a plan happily accepted.

They were brave enough to turn on the lights in the basement and examine the massive old furnace. "I think it was originally a sawdust furnace" Ward explained. "I believe the house was built before the Second World War." She warned him that she was very afraid of spiders and made him promise to protect her. "There seems to be a ton of room down here, but none of it is well utilized."

"You don't impress me as a guy who needs his man-cave," she said with a bit of a giggle, "with a cooler of beer and a large TV. But if this was cleared out and had some padded carpeting, with this easy access from the street, it could be a great place for yoga lessons." It was the beginning of creative suggestions.

On the main floor they agreed that the removal of a wall would open the kitchen in a more available way. She avoided any comments about his bedroom, perhaps because that kiss had lighted a bit of an amorous fire that was best left unexamined for the moment. The sitting room had lots of potential to become a decent sized office or study with a desk. They both were enjoying the exploration of possibilities.

Ward mused, "You know, it seems to me this place is situated just backwards. The front windows look out at Winona while the lake view, which I think is much more impressive, is out the back. There would be a ton of parking if the driveway was off SE 76th."

They were seated on the old weary sofa. Becky pulled her feet under her so she could face him more directly and began a serious conversation. "I really love spending time with you, the more the better. Do you feel that way too?"

Ward nodded and answered, "Yes, I do. It's hard for me to know where the lines are, it's so new and special. I can't recall what our long conversations are about, but at the time they all feel very important."

"Do you recall the conversation we had about the chair of relationship?" Ward nodded that he did. "You shared that your counselor had talked about the four supporting legs of trust, respect, loyalty and openness, elements of a healthy relationship. It was so visual I can remember it well." He nodded again. "I feel that you have helped me find and appreciate those qualities in us. Do you agree?"

"I certainly do," he said softly. "It's a bit scary for me because it is so new. I feel like you are in all my thoughts and I love it." He looked at her darling face for a long moment. Finally he said even more softly, "I think I'm trying to say I care for you to the point that only the words 'I love you' are sweet enough to express my feelings for you." His eyes studied her face.

She moved a bit closer to him and said in the same soft voice, "It's almost like you are reading my mind. When I saw how sweet you were to mom and Sophie, I knew you weren't just playing with me." She took his hand and finished her thought. "I feel that we were meant for each other." She was still, hoping that he would move toward her. To her surprise he stood and offered to help her up.

"My sweet friend, I don't know where this moment is pulling us. I think it is one we will remember for years. I want it to be one we are proud of. I'm afraid I might want to complicate it, so how about us walking around the lake. For a December day a light jacket is all we'll need and the exercise will be good for us."

She pulled him to her and gently kissed him. "You are my hero. You are protecting us. I'm already proud of you. It is easy to be carried away when our hearts are so content. I agree that a walk would be what the doctor ordered."

When they arrived at the Fisherman's Grill, Ward was immediately aware that the name suggested a much lesser restaurant. The men were in military styled jackets and the women were in black party dresses. There was nothing grill-like in the atmosphere. He smiled at the incongruence, happy that he had stopped at the bank to fill his wallet. Jay and Florence were waiting for them. They rose and smiling warmly, embraced them both.

Ward greeted them by saying, "I hope the rest of the evening is as satisfying as the welcoming." It was a splendid beginning. Their window table looked out into a dark night adorned only with the distant lights simmering on Puget Sound. Much closer, a lighted ferry was making its way into the dock. There was the expected casual conversation about Christmas and the dwindling vacation days before January third when classes would resume.

When the serving person took their drink order, three of them requested wine and Ward asked for a diet coke. Becky thought, "Darn, he is holding to his principles even in this setting!" She smiled knowing that her affection was still increasing for this gentle man.

Jay said, "Ward, my brother said he would give you a call tomorrow. Are you going to be around? Phillip can drive down in the afternoon to take a look, if you're still interested."

"I'm very interested," Ward answered with a chuckle. "Beck and I were there this afternoon trying to imagine what that sow's ear could be changed into. I chatted with my dad about it. He said that the close proximity to Aurora and downtown is ideal. He thinks there is about to be another big growth spurt in property values, so it is an advantageous time." Their drinks were served and Ward suspected that this casual conversation was not the reason Jay and Florence wanted to talk with them, so he asked, "What's up with you guys? Are you ready for next week?"

"Yeah," Jay answered with a grin. "I think I'm going to join the Tootsie Roll troops and see if I can duplicate your success."

"Buddy, you've got to mean it if you try. I'll bet your students will make you become a believer." He looked at Florence and said, "I just learned that I was not the totem we believed I was. You guys knew one another at Western. It looks like things are going well for you." He expected that might introduce the real subject.

Jay took a deep breath but Florence spoke first. "Ward, you are a totem. I meant every word I said to you, and without your presence, I'm not sure this careful man would have opened the door of his heart to me. So, thank you. I would never have guessed that our two tables could be such wonderful friends today."

Jay finally said, "That's what we want to talk to you about." Becky's knee pressed against Ward's. "We want your opinion about some thoughts we are having." Both Ward and Becky smiled warmly.

Florence said in a confidential voice, "Jay asked me if I would like to move in with him. I told him I would, but I thought my place is larger and more convenient to our schools. We want to know what you think about it." She waited for a reply to such a major question.

Becky answered almost immediately. "I am very happy for you both to have found love and affection. I have suspected there was something special going on between you. You both seem happier." She reached over to hold Florence's hand. She added, "Do you have family near that you can talk to about it?"

Jay answered, "Yes, some. Neither of us are very confident they will approve. Both of our families are broken, and neither are what we would call happy marital examples."

Ward said softly, "You chose to ask us instead. I feel very honored and at the same time completely unprepared to answer. I just got my first kiss ever, so I am no authority on relationships. I don't know any secret for lasting happiness, but I do know the secret to failure." That brought a startled expression to all three of his listeners. "Just try to please everyone. It can't be done; it will only bring failure." He reached across to take Jay's hand. "If you two are convinced it is the right thing to do, I encourage you to do it bravely. There will be critics for sure, and challenges. I have a hunch that there will be many more of your trusted friends and admirers who will applaud and support you. We'll be in the front of the line. You are smart and strong. You will work it out and I promise to give you each a Tootsie Roll on your anniversary."

Florence said with a relaxed chuckle, "Now that's funny." Looking first into Becky's eyes and then Wards, she said, "We want to build a fantastic relationship like you two are doing. We want what you have."

Becky allowed a tear to run down her cheek. "That's a very sweet compliment. You are the ones who can do it. I heard Ward say that our life is the canvas and we are the painters. You can make a beautiful masterpiece."

"The really important thing," Ward said leaning toward them, "Is that what you think about yourself is far more critical than what anyone else might think. Each happy day you share together is like a brick in a lovely shrine. Fifty years from now you will see how right you were today."

Looking tenderly at him Florence asked, "You just got your first kiss? I'm sorry for all the kisses that weren't delivered. I want to give you one out of gratitude. You are both very special friends." Their food was served and the conversation returned to the ordinary stuff, but each of them thought that these past few minutes were far from ordinary; they could be called life defining.

Giggles, a Second Try

Ward and Becky were the first to arrive at Giggles. They wondered if the others were caught up in vacation agendas. A few minutes later Sean and Sarah came in with Sam and Maria. Ward was surprised to see Terry Remington come in alone. It was his first time there. They were just in the process of adding another chair to table sixteen, when Greg and Frieda came in with Caroline. The four sat at table fifteen, wondering what they would do without Florence's leadership. Just before seven o'clock, Jay and Florence entered to the welcoming cheer of the other ten. Both tables were filled, drinks were served and the house lights dimmed.

As the first table number was called, Florence leaned back so she could assure table sixteen that they were not going to be called. "Let's just enjoy the evening," her comforting words were spoken. Two more tables were called and Ward was confident that she had been correct. She wasn't. "Let's hear from table…. Sixteen," the M.C. called. A startled Florence looked around at her friends. She hesitated, and then started to get up.

Ward, put his hand on her shoulder and said, "I've got this." He stood up, hoping that he was really as prepared as he thought he might be.

"Hey, it's the professor. Welcome back!" Lou handed him the mic saying, "It's open mic night at Giggles! Let's give the professor a warm welcome!" His words were gracious but his expression was disappointed. He hadn't been able to pull one over on Florence, his intended target.

"Good evening folks," Ward said graciously. He didn't want to start off with an apology for his first rough landing. These attending had forgotten him by now anyway. "I wonder if you were lucky enough to receive wisdom from your grandmother or grandfather. I did. I remember very clearly how one day sitting on the porch, he said, 'Ward, everybody needs somebody to be goofy with.' He said it in a way that seemed very important, so I gave it some thought.

"Just across the alley from our house lived a kid my age named Willie. He had a basketball hoop on the garage and we often spent time using it. I thought grandpa was referring to Willie as my goofing friend. Then one day Willie swiped a can of his dad's beer and a cigarette. We sat out there in the alley and drank that whole thing and shared puffs. We were goofing for sure. All of a sudden Willie seemed to turn green and he puked on me, which made me puke right back on him." The room erupted with laughter. When they settled down a bit, he continued, "He cried a lot and I guessed we were not meant to goof around any more.

"But just down on the corner there was a girl named Patty, who I suspected might be my someone. All summer long we talked and rode bikes together. I noticed that she was developing some muscles on her chest much different than mine. One afternoon when we were alone I asked her if I could see them. They were a curiosity to me. She said she would show me hers if I showered her mine. 'That's a deal,' I said bravely and I unbuttoned my shirt and opened it so she could see my skinny white chest. She called me 'stupid', and hit me with a book." There was more sustained laughter. "I knew she was not the goofy one for me either.

"I decided I might have to expand my search to worldwide, so when I was in high school there was Bess. She was from Ballard and spoke with a strange accent. She was some sort of a diesel mechanic or something. She told me she worked at Marshalls in women's underwear. That was something I wanted to see. When I walked in she was busy sizing. She would pull a pair of panties on her head and say, 'Desie'l fitter, you bet'cha. Yust right.'" The audience groaned at the corny joke. "It was obvious that she was not my goofy friend. I had to expand my search area even larger.

I found Gerta in Leavenworth working at a café. I could remember her name, Gerta, because her skirta was very short and those cute legs suggested we could be goofy together. When I asked her what time she got off work so we could be goofy together, she said, 'Nein!' Since it was seven, I was happy to wait a couple hours. I didn't know she was speaking German. I could have a couple beers and learn the local dance while I was waiting. It really didn't matter that she had said, 'No' because by nine o'clock I was buzzed and doing the chicken dance in the street... naked! The nice policeman let me sleep it off in a room at his jail. Gerta wasn't the one either. But I didn't give up.

I signed up for ski lessons at Snoqualmie. The instructor was super cute and with a smile she told me she was a cougar. I thought that meant she was hitting on me so we could be goofy together. At the end of the lesson I tried to give her a kiss. It was not a good idea in subfreezing weather. My tongue froze to her lip and the ski patrol had to pour hot coffee on it to melt me. I was asked to go home and not come back.

"I decided that grandpa had given me bad advice. Some people just don't have anyone to be goofy with." The light turned yellow, just as Ward had planned. "I teach at a high school and had resigned myself to a goof-less fate. Then one of my colleagues invited me to come to Giggles with them and low and behold I discovered that there are hundreds of you. Folks who are goofy and like it and will let me be goofy too. Happy New Year you goofers and may we all have a goofy New Year too." His light turned red and there was a generous mix of applause and laughter.

As Ward returned to table sixteen, all eleven of his friends stood, applauding. Florence said, "Now that was very funny. She embraced him and kissed his cheek, but Becky held him and kissed his lips in a lingering tribute. The others continued to hoot and turned the applause toward her.

Eventually Florence asked, "Did your grandfather really give you that material, or did you create it?

Ward had a huge satisfied smile as he said, "The idea came from Becky. I just polished it a bit. She's my muse. I never knew my grandfather." As the hour came to an end, Ward invited them back to his bachelor cave. "I have a couple bottles of wine, some beer and hot chocolate if anyone is interested. They all wanted to continue their evening and were especially happy that Terry would join them.

"Good morning my very special friend." Ward's phone call was always a happy sound to Becky. "Are you awake for the whole day? I hope this isn't too early to call." His voice was warm and welcome. "I just got the call from Jay's brother, Phillip. He said he has time to see the place at about 2 o'clock, depending on traffic. Would you and your mom like to get some fish and chips for lunch? I think I heard that Sophie would be home this evening. I'll bet you have missed her."

"I've been up for hours," Becky lied. "And I'll bet you have missed her almost as much. I'll ask mom about lunch and call you right back, after I shower and get dressed." They both had a fun chuckle.

The door chimes rang at five minutes before two. Ward said, "He is starting well, one point for promptness." Moments later he introduced Phil Taylor to Becky.

"I feel like we are already friends," the contractor said brightly, "I've heard so much about you from Jay." He opened his laptop computer and asked, "Let's start with what you want. What is your vision for this renovation?"

"To tell you the truth, Phil, I'm open to just about any suggestions. I got this place a couple years ago in a distress sale, and would never have looked twice at it if it were not for the bargain price. I have sort of imagined this as a rambler with a daylight basement and upstairs. I just live in the middle now. I think it would be great to have an office or study on this level and maybe a family room or media room." He looked at Becky. "You had an idea of a more useable basement for a yoga room."

She gave a bit of a nod and added, "Its location is so ideal I think there could be several uses for it."

Phil said, "I'll tell you what, let me wander around for a few minutes and see what you have here. Are there any rooms upstairs that I shouldn't open? I haven't seen any sign of a dog. Is there anything I might disturb?"

Ward answered, "There are no critters. I'm the only one who lives here, so most of the upstairs is empty."

As Phil investigated, Ward introduced a new subject that took Becky by complete surprise. "Steve just told me about a time-share they have in Maui. They rarely use it and often just give away its availability. There are three bedrooms and it is only a short walk to the beach. Do you think your mom and Sophie would like to go all together during spring break? Our only expense would be airfare, a car rental and groceries. Would you like to think about it, or is it too goofy? Am I stretching my luck?" A large smile was on Becky's delighted face.

She embraced him first. Then she said softly against his cheek, "Most girls who get an invitation to go on spring break are part of a romantic plan. You sweetheart you, mom and Sophie were first on the list for clarity." She kissed his cheek.

"I'll accept the praise, but remember there are three girls in the family that I am trying to woo. I can be a pretty decent romantic."

"As it happens," Becky said with a happy grin, "Sophie's ninth birthday is during the break. "Wouldn't it be fun to do something special for her?" They talked about it with growing enthusiasm for about ten minutes. Finally Phil came back in. He was shaking his head with a large grin.

"Oh boy" he began. "This old place has amazing possibilities! I like to take my first look without knowing your budget. That way I am thinking the sky is the limit. Jay told you that we can line this up with the Home and Garden television series and they will share much of the cost. To do that we will need to at least reno all of this level. We can replace the roofing and paint the outside. The interior could take out a couple walls, replace the windows with double pane and insulate the walls for efficiency, replace the electrical, replace the water heater, furnace and add air conditioning. I noticed there is no fireplace. We could add a gas one. With new lighting and restored floors, which are in great condition by the way, this old girl would be very attractive. That's level one.

"Second level reno would address the basement. The ceiling down there was surprisingly high. I'm not sure how long it has been since the little single garage was used, if ever. I'll bet they just used street parking and kept the garage for storage. There is enough room down there for either a second apartment, a daycare center, or a huge media room. It would only need insulation for sound, a new bathroom, new electrical, floor covering and a ton of can lights. That's level two reno.

"Now level three gets way exciting, and remember these are just raw ideas. We need a concept before we start looking at numbers. From the front of the house, nothing will change, except doing away with the garage door and driveway, leveling the yard and improving curb appeal with a covered porch and some fresh landscaping. But how about adding a twenty by sixty addition," his voice almost broke into a giggle, "to the back of the house, basement and first level? In the basement that could be a three car garage accessed from 76th and more space to be utilized. On the main level that could be a large family room, an impressive media room and a killer office study. A kitchen pantry could be added, and move the laundry there too. All that east facing wall would have large double pane windows to see the lake. The cherry on top," he paused for just a moment, "would be a large railed sky patio, with access from second floor French doors. To pass the building code it would probably need an outside stairway, which would offer extra safety as a fire escape. The upstairs would use one of those small bedrooms for another bathroom with pocket doors, and an complete replacement of the bath that is there now." He took a deep breath and said finally, "Oh, I would also see the entire backyard blacktopped for easy access to the garage and excess parking, and a chain-link fence behind a Photinia hedge for security.

Phil concluded, "Ward, remember that my job is to think about spectacular renovation that would increase Home and Garden ratings. This is probably more than you would normally choose to do. But it will be a very generous offer to you that would create a legacy. There won't be anything like it in North Seattle, I guarantee." There were several questions from both Ward and Becky. Finally Phil shared that his wife, Gwen, was an interior stager for several realtors in the Bellingham area and had good contacts with consignment furnishings and the Overstock liquidations. For a very reasonable price, she could help make the new place beautiful inside. He promised to get back to Ward with some drawings and numbers by the end of next week.

As Becky was making her way toward the door, she said, "The scope and design of his suggestions are almost more than I can imagine. The really exciting thing is I get to ask mom and Sophie if they want to go to Hawaii. She gave him a warm hug and a little kiss. She wanted to do more but felt that later might be a better time for that.

Ward went upstairs and tried to envision Phil's suggestions; he went out to the back yard trying to do it there as well. He paced off twenty strides and determined that was about the full width of the proposed extension. Then he called Nora to invite himself to dinner with them. He so needed grounded wisdom to help him see this as either a remarkable possibility or a colossal mistake.

The dishes were cleared and Steve and Nora had poured a glass of wine for themselves. Ward laughed when he told them that he was sticking with diet Coke diet. He told them about the conversation with Becky about the Maui possibility, and they both expressed delight that the relationship had grown to this level.

Ward giggled and told them that amidst all the fun presents he had received for Christmas the one outstanding in his mind was Becky's kiss. "I finally feel like an entire person, with a heart that yearns for more." That made Nora come around the table and give him a warm embrace. Then they agreed that securing the date for the condo's use would be of first importance.

Steve had just asked about Ward's finances. "You say you own the house free and clear, just utilities, phone, cable, taxes and insurance?" When Ward nodded, he went on, "No car payment, school debts or other payments?"

Ward shook his head. "After the mess I made of Spokane," he said with a shrug, "I've been a radical conservative with my money. There is still over thirty thousand from the settlement and sale of the farm in savings and there is about a third of that in my checking. I figured that if teaching is a flop again, I can get by until I get a real job."

Nora chuckled, "If this semester is any indication, your savings are safe."

Steve stayed with the question. "What is your take-home each month, about three thousand?" When Ward nodded agreement, his dad went on, "For an average budget that should be able to satisfy a house payment of about $800 a month. By the time taxes and insurance are factored in, you should be able to handle a loan of just under a hundred and sixty thousand. That would go a long way to make your place a home to be proud of."

"Phil, the reno guy, has told me that this could be far more impressive than just something to be proud of. It could be a bell-ringer."

Steve was having a moment of fatherly pride. This young man, who had overcome so much, seemed humble in light of their conversation. "Ward, I am so very proud of what you are doing. You have surpassed every expectation and still you have your feet on solid ground. I couldn't be more proud of you. When you get those numbers about costs, let's talk some more about this. I have a Rotary friend, Craig Jensen, at Washington Mutual, who just happens to be a fan of yours. You caught his attention with your speech to the club. I'll bet if I agree to co-sign with you, we can make it happen. If you want to go for it."

"I have to admit that I am living in an intoxicating atmosphere of pure anticipation. Becky is principle in that of course and all this other just adds to it. I don't want to put a curse on it, but worst case scenario, if I take this reno leap and can't make it, the house will sell for at least double what I have in it. That's a pretty safe risk." He asked them to say little about the plans tomorrow evening at dinner.

NEW YEAR'S EVE

Nora was so concentrating on the game she was playing with Sophie that she had to be reminded that she had a tray in the oven.

Steve said in a humorous voice, "Sweetheart the Crabby Puffs are about to catch fire!" Actually they were just golden brown and perfect. But it brought her into the kitchen quickly.

The house was festive and eager to greet one more guest. Still, they all turned toward the door at the sound of the doorbell. He was taller than Lois expected. In gray slacks, a white mock-turtle neck and a blue blazer he was thoughtfully dressed for the occasion. His salt and pepper hair with dark eyebrows made Lois catch her breath. He was far more handsome than she expected and when they shook hands in greeting she was tempted not to let go.

Steve chuckled as he read the happy greeting between the two. "Nothing makes me happier than to see two of my good friends becoming better friends."

Nora gave him a happy poke and answered, "Nick our home is happier when you are in it. If we can get this lazy host to get the fruit plate out of the frig, we'll be all set." She had prepared an elegant feast in an atmosphere of celebration as the calendar turned to a fresh year.

When the bowls and platter were finally emptied and the dishes were cleared, Steve asked a question to encourage conversation. "What was a highlight from the past year for you?"

Ward was seated to his left so he answered first, "I think the Tootsie Rolls have been a surprising boost to my classes."

Becky was seated next to him and after a reflective moment she continued the sharing, "I'm grateful for Giggles and the new friends it has brought us."

Sophie looked at her mom for a nod signaling her turn. "I really liked it when Ward came to my caroling program. I think he liked it and that made me real happy." The adults all smiled at her sweet innocence.

Nora spoke with a voice choked with emotion. "There have been many highlights in my year. Having you at this table tonight is the finest, I believe."

Lois also choked back some tender emotion as she replied, "It has been a long time since I have had this much joy. After years of sadness we are very grateful for this family fullness that Ward started and now you folks are completing."

Nick, who was in the presence of brand new friends answered safely. "I heard from Jackson, my son just last week. I don't know where he is but I know he is safe." He thought for just a moment and added, "I think being welcomed and embraced by you at this table is nearly as wonderful."

Steve's gaze held Nora's for a moment before he answered, "Twelve years ago we opened our home and hearts to Ward. Tonight those hearts are overflowing with gratitude that our table is overflowing with affection." He surrendered to the wave of emotion, struggling to control his voice. "Now what are you anticipating in the New Year?" He looked at Ward with a growing smile.

"Well I'm hoping..." Ward's grin suggested that there were several conclusions to the thought.... "that I can have my old room again for about three months while my old place gets reborn." He chuckled nervously.

Becky's smile grew even larger. "I'm hoping I finally get to see Hawaii and learn to hula." She waved her hands over her head from side to side.

Sophie joined her mom's smile saying, I've never been on an airplane, and I've never seen a turtle. Maybe we can do both for my birthday." She waved her arms just like her mom.

Nora shook her head as she said, "I don't know what more I can hope for; all of my dreams have come true. Perhaps we can attend a church service some Sunday together."

Her smile was most appreciated by Lois, who answered her with the hope that whatever affection was at this table would just continue to grow. She gave a shy glance toward Nick.

Nick was obviously feeling the tenderness of the table too as he said, "I so enjoy being a part of this circle. I certainly don't want to wait a whole year before I get to be with you all again. Perhaps you will honor me by being my guests at Salty's on Alki for a Saturday brunch. My cooking skills are limited to thaw and heat." He looked at Sophie and added, "They have a chocolate fountain for dipping marshmallows or strawberries." In that moment he sounded just like a grandpa.

The meal finished with Nora's special dessert, a vanilla mousse stuffed crepe with raspberry port topping. Then folks chatted in the family room waiting for the televised fireworks from the east coast. Nora and Sophie finished their game and the seven diners agreed that this had been a memorable celebration, each for a different reason. Not once was the old house reno mentioned.

As leave-taking was beginning at the door, Nick held Lois's hand and thanked her for a most enjoyable evening. She agreed and said there would be many happy thoughts because of the evening. He also shook Ward's hand and praised him for overcoming such challenges.

Ward's response became a repeated phrase. He said, "I have come to believe the only people I want to get even with are those who have blessed me." As he said it his eyes were holding those of Becky's. It was about to become a very happy New Year indeed.

She called him in the morning. "Good morning Sleepy Head." It was before 8 o'clock. "Sophie and I would like to walk around the lake. Would you like to join us?"

"Sweetie, have you looked outside? It's raining. We would need foul weather clothes." He didn't want to say "no" but this idea was silly so early in the day.

"O.K. then," she said brightly, "may we come over and explore your old house again?" Her laughter was like a breath of affection. "Sophie learned to play Chinese checkers last night. Nora gave it to her and she wonders if she can show you how to play. We both want to play with you." Again her little chuckle warmed his heart. As it turned out they played through the morning, took Lois with them for lunch at Spud's Fish and Chips, and went to a matinee movie about a lost boy and the dog that helped find his way home. Sophie said that someday she would have a dog like that if it would like Silvia.

Monday was still a holiday, but one spent house cleaning, doing laundry and grocery shopping for the week. It was back to the routine, with one exception; they had to take Silvia to the doctor. She was weak and unsteady. Lois said she was afraid that the years had caught up with her. Her diagnosis may have been vague, but her prognosis was accurate. The little gray kitty was too weak to survive. Ward drove over to try to console a heartbroken child and a distraught household. There is so little that can be said, yet it is so important to be a tender supportive presence. He presented Sophie a soft stuffed animal that looked very much like a Silvia, even to the shiny green glass eyes. He said, "Memories are meant to be kept in the heart, but sometimes it helps if they can be held in your arms too."

Sophie's tears dampened the head of the toy as she held it tightly and Becky embraced Ward in a grateful hug.

Tuesday was the return of school students. Ward had four new ones now there were 94. Wednesday Peggy Jameson called to confirm that the Sunday evening caucus meeting had two spaces reserved for them and Ward assured her that he was eager to see them again. Thursday was Giggles with all twelve in attendance and the assurance from Florence that they would not be called upon. She had a blunt conversation with Lou, warning him to knock off the surprises if he wanted their continued business.

Friday UPS delivered a packet of drawings, descriptions and work schedule along with an estimate of the cost of the renovation! Ward asked Nora if they could all have supper with them and explore the scope of this decision. Each night before turning out the lights, Ward and Becky chatted on the phone, sharing the challenges of the day and the joy of the other's companionship. The "love" word was not used again, but it was definitely implied often.

On the way into the city center, Becky asked Ward, "What do you suppose we will be asked to discuss. I hardly feel like a source of information." She looked at him with something between confusion and interest. He often came up with an aspect of a discussion that made her think.

"I suppose there will be interest in reducing the size of government, or the challenge of race relations, or dealing with a growing homeless element, or taxes, or gun control and violence in our streets, or a burgeoning immigration challenge. They are all hot buttons and next November will be a crucial voting season." His expression had lost its smile. These were serious problems.

"Ward, you amaze me." she said affectionately. "You always seem to come up with a fresh viewpoint that leads to a solution or compromise. I don't know how you do it, but you seem to find a rainbow in the storm. Even when I don't quite agree with you, I am forced to admit that your suggestions deserve a second thought, You're good!"

"Thanks, I need that encouragement going into a room full of political bias. I'd rather have a root canal." She chuckled and carefully hooked her arm in his.

Ward had not been in the Sheraton. His first impression was that of elegance and modern beauty. "This is breathtaking," he said quietly to Becky, who agreed and guided them into the third floor banquet room. They knew their table assignment and saw Peggy standing near it.

She waved and welcomed them to the evening. "Bob is at the bar, fortifying himself for an experience he really does not enjoy. There are so many opposing attitudes he is exhausted by the time we go home." She embraced Becky and shook Ward's hand warmly. "You are going to help him enjoy the evening. He thinks the world of you both."

As she was speaking a well dressed man with an even more handsome smile approached Ward saying, "It has been seven years, but I recognize the best speaker we ever had at Rotary." He offered his hand to Peggy and Becky as well. Then he introduced himself. "I'm Craig Jensen. I have lunch with your dad every Wednesday at Rotary. He crows your praise regularly and just told me you have a construction task that is exciting. I'm the manager of the University Washington Mutual. If you don't already have a lender for the project, come in and see me. It sounds like a challenge we would welcome."

The lights dimmed and the M.C. asked folks to find their places. A Chaplain led a prayer of gratitude with a bit of patriotic flavor, then a lovely lady lead the singing of the National Anthem and the pledge of allegiance. While the evening's power presenters were introduced, the servers began distributing a grand meal. Dr. Robert made introductions around the table of ten. He explained that each table would share their ideas on an assigned current subject. Peggy was the recorder for this table and would send their wisdom into the central office to be combined into general observations. It was an easy way to know the mood of the GOP in the Seattle area. "Our topic," he said confidentially, "is gun control. The Democrats are pushing hard for some new legislation to modify the second amendment."

The first speaker talked about the challenge of being a minority party at the moment and ways of utilizing available communication tools. The second speaker outlined shifts in the values of the young voters. Changes in financial pressures and living patterns were strong factors for consideration. A four step process was suggested to increase their involvement. The third one reached Ward's heart with a call to patriotic zeal. His premise was that the Democrats had lost the passion of unity that formed our young nation and made us a strong world power. Ward would like to have heard him say more. But it was time for table talk. A brief break was offered for those who needed a bar or bathroom visit. The sound system played My Country 'tis of Thee while folks were milling about. For most tables the discussion started immediately.

The lady sitting next to Dr. Robert said, "I believe all guns should be outlawed. We don't live in the wild west anymore.

The lady sitting next to her agreed and added, "If criminals get caught with a gun they should be sent to prison to put some teeth in the prohibition."

The next was a man who said, "I have a gun and it gives me some assurance that I could protect my family from an intruder." His smile was more apologetic than confident.

The next was also a man who said quietly, "Of course I would try to protect my family. But nothing I own is worth killing someone else to preserve it. Let them take it. We will either get it back or replace it. No, I would never use a gun against another human being.

A woman was the next to speak and she said flatly, "I hate guns, even the idea of them. I think they should all be destroyed, not just made illegal."

The man sitting next to Becky said, I don't know if I could use a gun against an intruder of my home, but I'm pretty sure if someone broke in, it would be too late to get the protection I might need. I have a gun and I'm stuck on the fence.

Becky said, I'm not. I hate guns and the violence that surrounds them. I think there should be a law against them. Maybe that means an attacker would use a baseball bat instead. Our civilized world has laws against violence." Her chin quivered and Ward understood the cause of it.

Ward was quiet for just a moment before answering, "I don't own a gun and don't expect I ever will. But that's not the point of the question. The last word in the second amendment is 'infringed'. Most defenders of that second amendment feel a sacred inalienable right to bear arms, which must not be infringed. I think handguns are meant to shoot people and so should be illegal to own. But the fourth word of the amendment is 'militia', and anyone who owns a gun is declaring that he or she is willing to volunteer to be part of the 'well regulated security of our free state.' I salute their willingness and believe they should be armed to do it."

Peggy smiled at Ward's fresh concept. "I also hate guns and am afraid of them. I would be happy if they had never been invented, but that is too simplistic. I think their time is passed."

Dr. Robert was the last at the table to speak. Looking at Ward he said, "All of us would agree that the use of a gun against someone is wrong. But you have raised a whole new concept. A volunteer militia that arms itself could be a societal advantage." His smile grew larger as he thought about it. "A militia could stand against unruly protesters in support of local police. In emergencies they could help battle wild fires. It is a provocative notion, but how could you find out who owns a gun at this late date. There are millions." His question was directed only at Ward.

Ward shrugged, saying gently, "It's not the gun that's dangerous, but the bullets that it fires. Bullets have a shelf life or are expended and must be replaced. If the sale of ammunition was regulated and carefully recorded, a list of owners would be developed and knowledge of the kind of gun they have would grow. If the owner was unwilling to volunteer, which might be fairly common, he or she would simply buy no more ammunition at least. Perhaps they would choose to get rid of the gun and there would be fewer available to injure others." He shrugged again.

Dr. Robert had an appreciative smile as he said, "Ward, you have reminded us that there are several answers to every question. We're going to make sure that Director Suzanne sees this and I am sure she will want to speak with you more about it."

Ward thought to himself, "One dinner and two significant contacts; some folks would call that a success!" He was not sure of that conclusion.

On the way home they had a lot to talk about, highlights of the evening. Becky said, "I feel that patriotism is more important to me now, as it is to you. I was reminded how lax I have been. It was fun to be in that group of power people."

"I agree," Ward said. "I recognized Director Murphy from her years on the evening news. It feels incongruous to have a celebrity as Director of a political party."

"I think she is acting Director, but she is also a candidate for the King County Executive spot next year. She is a pretty powerful lady," Becky added, "Especially a pretty lady." Ward nodded in agreement.

Becky changed the subject, knowing that they would soon be home. "Have you thought much about the renovation? Do you think it's going to happen?"

"For sure it's going to happen," Ward said with a grin. "The real question is, how much of a renovation will happen? I promised Phil I would get back to him this week. He said it would take two to six weeks to get a permit and then eight to ten weeks to do the work if we go with the whole plan. That could be by the time school is out for the summer"

Becky asked, "How are you feeling about that?"

"My head tells me that it is a no-miss investment if the Home and Garden folks come through. "My heart wonders what I would want to do with all that space. It would more than double the size of this already large old shell."

"May I make a suggestion?" she asked softly.

"Oh Beck, you know how I value your insight and support," he whispered affectionately. "Sure, suggest away."

"Have you heard about the increase or decrease of desire?" Her voice had taken on a more enthused force. When Ward repeated, "desire?,' she elbowed him and said, "Not that kind. You know, 'Is it right or is it wrong? Is it good or bad?, that kind of desire." When he nodded, she continued, "Let's get our folks to help us pray each day morning, noon and night for the increase or decrease. By Wednesday it will be clear what you should do. Do you want to try that?" Her face was intent and he was convinced that it was a serious question to her, so it was a serious answer she was looking for.

"This will be a new challenge for me," he said sincerely, "but a very interesting one. I'm in! Tell me how it works."

"Do you mean what words should you use?" When he nodded, she smiled that happy way and said, "Try thanking God first for this wonderful opportunity, then say, 'Lord, open my heart and my mind to see what this project may do for you. Guide me in your will and show me. Amen.' That's enough. Repeat it several times if you want. If it gets cold and corny, you will understand a decrease of desire. But if it becomes more exciting, you will know the increase and want to go ahead full speed. I heard Dr. Jameson say, 'Fence-sitting is the devil's ally.' You won't want to do that."

He asked with a grin, "Are you going to ask your mom and Sophie to join in the prayer experiment? Should I ask Steve and Nora too?"

"Well sure!" she said happily because she knew this was a fresh concept for Ward. "We are your team! Full power, Family power!" Her exuberance was contagious.

As soon as he got home he called Steve and shared the suggestion Becky had made. Both he and Nora agreed to be part of the experiment. So when the light was turned off and he was under the covers he spoke out loud to the Lord words of gratitude, and the request, 'Guide me – show me". In the following three days it was repeated often.

The next afternoon just as the fourth period class was leaving Ward was still thinking about the experiment when a lot of shouting was drawing a crowd in the hall. He hurried to see the nature of the problem. There was a heated argument focusing on the ownership of a cell phone. Paul Brock was contending that the phone Ted Lawson had just taken from his pocket was stolen from him. There was a bit of a struggle to take it away from the taller young man. Frankly, Ward thought the ruckus was more a desire on the crowd's part to get rid of some holiday energy so he stepped into the mêlée and told everyone to settle down. He didn't mean to shout "Please!" but that is sort of how it came out. He held out his hand signaling Ted to surrender the phone.

"That's my phone," Paul declared. "I know it's mine!"

Ted answered just as forcefully, "I just got it for Christmas, you Jerk." He surrendered it his teacher.

"Look on the back of it, Paul insisted. "There is a big scratch where I dropped it." He was confident his phone would be returned.

Ward turned the phone over to expose a shiny flaw-free back cover. "Doesn't seem scratched to me", he said. Showing it to Paul he asked, "Does this still seem like your beat up phone?"

Quietly a contrite accuser said, "No. I was wrong." Looking at his classmate he said, "I'm sorry for the trouble man. I really thought it was…."

Just then Abe Tom, the vice principal arrived to "break up the fight". "What's going on here?" he asked briskly. Reading the positioning of everyone he pointed at the two who had already settled the dispute. "Come with me, you two." It was just his intent to take them downstairs to cool off.

Ward started to intervene but was bluntly thanked for breaking up the mess. As it turned out, Principal J. J. Reese suspended the two young men for two weeks as punishment for fighting. You know how there is more to an iceberg than what we can see? Before the day was over, Mr. Reese's office was the scene of considerable conflict. Four parents came in to protest the unusual reaction for a simple argument. Mr. Reese stood his ground suggesting that it would be a lesson in behavior for them. He was sticking to his decision.

Then the basketball coach came to the office to ask, "What in the world are you thinking Jim? We just made the metro quarter finals and you have suspended my best forward and second half center? Do you know how ridiculous that is?"

Mr. Reese warned the coach to watch his language or he might join them in suspension. Obviously there was no logic or compassion available.

Before the afternoon was over, Ted Lawson's dad returned to Mr. Reese's office to ask once again for some understanding. A simple disagreement could not in good conscience merit such drastic action. His son was counting on a scholarship. If he was out for two games Roosevelt might not go to the finals and his son might not get to go to the U. His plea was denied so he said, "You really are a cocky little rooster. I'd like to teach you some management skills."

Mr. Reese said simply, "Bring it! I'd like to expel your kid too."

Before the day was over the School Superintendent heard complaints from two families and intervened on their behalf.

The rain turned serious on Tuesday and the snow began Wednesday morning. During the early morning hours it accumulated enough for schools to be cancelled. He called Becky wondering if this was a part of the sign. She assured him that in her experience the Lord didn't work like that, but it was a fine opportunity to poll the team for their observations.

"As for me," Becky said strongly, "I sense a very positive increase of enthusiasm for both you and the project." She chuckled and said, "For sure more for you! Mom and Sophie are happy to join me in that feeling. You get three yeses from us."

He called Nora and was told that because the main streets were still pretty clear, Steve had gone into his office. She added that the exercise of prayer had been quite interesting for them because they both changed from questioning the timing of this project to being one hundred percent convinced that it was a great thing to do. She said that the deeper part of their experience was a desire to talk a lot more about the increase of desire between them for a more spiritual element in their home. After talking with her just a bit about some of the details, he called Phil and confirmed that the full renovation was a marvelous opportunity. "The full team gave me a green light, so it's a for sure go for the full three stage reno!" Ward said happily. "Now I wonder what the next step should be."

Phil said jubilantly, "Fantastic news! This is perfect timing. I can apply for the renovation permit online. If you can have your portion of the finances ready by the end of the month Home and Garden will have theirs. Their policy is that you will be responsible for the first third, then they will be in for the next third and you divide the balance when the job is finished. I'll start lining up subs. Will you be able to be out of the house by the end of the month? It's going to get real empty real quick." His voice broke into a happy chuckle.

Ward joined him in delight, saying, "You're making this very easy to begin. I can be moved to dad's place by the end of next week. I'm holding my breath that it will really be that easy to completion."

"Me too," the contractor agreed. "When I told Jay about your plans, he said a June wedding on the sky patio would be superb. I don't suppose he's had an opportunity to ask you, but I'm feeling a bit more invested in this project now. It's not only going to be splendid, but personal as well." Several more inches of snow fell during the night and the school district announced that all schools would be closed for the remainder of the week. Florence sent emails to the folks saying that she felt Giggles would be skipped for a week. With little to do, Ward finished reading Tom Brokaw's book, The Greatest Generation and reclaimed the moving boxes from the basement. He began packing the nonessential things, which were just about everything. He smiled to himself as he even had a pile that would be donated to Goodwill instead of moved again. He also talked to Becky at least twice a day.

By Saturday morning the streets were slushy but still a snowy mess to drive on. Becky called to say she missed him so much she was thinking about hiking to his house. He told her that was a dangerous idea, not because of the hazards of the roads but his pent up emotions of cabin fever might pounce on her on sight.

She giggled and said, "I wish!"

Just before noon there was a knock on his door and for just a moment he thought, "My gosh, she has done it!" At least he was glad that he had used a strong piece of plywood to clear the snow from the sidewalk so the mailman could deliver the mail. Opening the door he greeted a distinguished group. Dr. Jameson, Craig Jensen and Suzanne Murphy were smiling at him!

"Am I ever in trouble!" he said playfully. Opening the door fully, he invited them in. At least the house was warm, even though there were scant furnishings. The men shook his hand before introducing him to Mrs. Murphy. They asked if he had a few minutes to chat about a proposal.

"I've been snowbound for days!" Ward joked with a husky voice. "You are the first living persons I've seen in days, so please take as much time as you'd like." Good natured chuckles responded to his humor. He invited them to be seated at the dining room table where there were four chairs.

Mr. Jensen looked around saying, "Now I see the scope and potential of this renovation. It really is in an ideal location. Ward, thank you for moving your banking accounts to Washington Mutual. It made the approval of your funding a slam dunk." Ward was happy to get that news. "Do I understand there will be some added space?"

"Yes, a considerable addition, actually," Ward responded cheerily. "The plans are to add a twenty by sixty foot addition to this east side, both basement and main floor. The top of that will be a sky patio accessed from upstairs. Downstairs will have a couple new rooms and a very large commons area. Becky has suggested yoga lessons might utilize it. This level will have a new open concept and a family room, a study or office and a media room. It's an exciting proposal." Ward was beginning to feel awkward wondering about the purpose of this visit.

Suzanne asked him, "How did you feel about the caucus meeting the other night? We were lucky to get it in before the snow."

Ward answered, "Being our first opportunity, the evening was delightful. There was a fresh patriotism that we found stimulating. The informative part was interesting and being in your presence was very charming. You are a celebrity that we can be very proud to claim. The Jameson's are also super impressive folks, as is my dad's Rotary brother, my new banker. The whole evening was terrific." He hoped that was a good beginning.

Dr. Robert replied, "We have been very impressed with you as well Ward. You are an outstanding teacher and pretty sharp as a stand up too. And your insightful addition to our table conversation brought a whole new aspect to a difficult subject. You were positive and helpful." He smiled warmly and Ward was convinced he meant it.

Suzanne said, "These gentlemen escorted me here to offer you a bit of a proposal and a plan that is just in the formative stage, like your impressive renovation idea. Our state has had a Democratic bias for too long. To change that I think we need a more personal strategy. I've suggested that we go to the basic neighborhood network idea, getting neighbors gathered and informed about crucial issues. To work, that plan needs two important elements, someplace to meet, and someone to shepherd the plan. We are aiming at Seattle, Spokane, Olympia, of course and Vancouver to begin. I would rejoice if we could have a network in every significant city in the state. The model would have each zip code gather as a group. We have the registered voters in each area that we could contact and invite to an annual gathering, twelve a year so there would be a different one each month. The shepherd's task would be to turn on the lights, open the door and welcome the neighborhood. Eventually I think it would build community if each neighborhood also received some sort of news update and reminder at least once a quarter. With a stronger neighborhood base, I think the GOP would have a stronger presence in the political arena.

"Part of my proposal, Ward, is that you accept the part time shepherd position for the Seattle area. The salary is a thousand dollars a month, which is probably less than the job indicates. My staff can give you a list of names of the leaders or currently active people in each neighborhood. They could help with a strategy to reach more. We will provide you with a computer for connectivity, a distribution list and whatever office supplies you need to do a quality job. It will start small and grow. We want folks to know that we mean business.

"The second part of our proposal is the reason we battled the elements to come to you today. You are just in the design phase of this renovation. If there could be two office spaces downstairs with easy access, one for me and one for the shepherd, and a room large enough to seat the neighborhood gatherings of about a hundred people, we would have a great chance of success. If there were public restroom facilities, we would reimburse you another thousand dollars a month. In addition we would provide the chairs and a large screen TV and a DVD player to share information." She looked at the two other men and asked, "Isn't that about what we agreed?" When they nodded, she turned back toward Ward and said sincerely, "I hope you'll consider both, favorably." He was aware that her brown eyes were steady and mesmerizing.

Mr. Jensen, his banker, said, "If you need a side business, I'll bet you could do a lot of weddings in such a convenient and charming place."

Ward chuckled, "That's funny. It's the second time I have heard that suggestion. I need to become a Justice of the Peace to conduct them."

Now Mr. Jensen's smile grew even larger. "Washington State hasn't had Justices for several years. Now they are called Clerks of the Court with marriage authority. You can, with an attorney's recommendation and the sum of thirty five dollars, file your name and conduct weddings. Those online ordinations are simply clerks of the court."

Suzanne brought them back to the subject at hand. "Ward, I believe you could become a very important part of the Washington GOP. It could begin right here, right now. Please consider this request. If you are not interested in being Seattle's shepherd, whether you conduct weddings or not, please consider making your basement space available to us. We really need a convenient and gracious place to meet and I have some energetic plans for the fall that will also need some gathering availability. That will be a separate proposal later. Mr. Jensen has pointed out that the reimbursement, which is not taxable, would pretty much pay for your entire renovation." She knew how to play rough.

Ward promised to respond to the offer by Tuesday, explaining that he needed to get the counsel of his family. Dr. Robert understood that included Miss Rhodes. Suzanne thanked him for his interest and gave him one of her business cards. Then the trio went back out into the drizzly morning mess and Ward had somethin new to pray about.

He immediately called Steve to glean his wisdom on the request. When Nora heard the scope of the two offers, she said that she would fix a spaghetti dinner for six if he wanted to have all his girls in on the discussion. Ward smiled as he said, "You're a pretty wise mom. You understand how much I like those folks, and how much more I need them. Do you want to invite them or should I?"

"I'll be happy to do that," Nora confided. "I have another Chinese checker board that Sophie might be happy to use."

The conversation with Steve lasted longer than Ward had expected. It ended with Steve offering to develop a list of incentive drawings from his advertising budget at the dealership to accompany the first few neighborhood meetings. "We have all sorts of items like sound systems, tires, tune-ups or detailing that might draw in an initial attendance. It could be good for both of us." Once again Ward was grateful for the affectionate support of the Harts.

Even before the serious conversation began Ward knew the evening had been a success. The congenial bond between them was growing with each opportunity to be together. Finally Ward shared with them the surprising offer he had received and the impact it could have on the expensive renovation.

Nora was the first to offer an observation. "It seems to me that it is most inviting now. I just wonder if there should be some time limits, you know, like an annual lease that could be considered and renewed. It might start to feel to the ones who are using the space that a form of ownership is implied."

Becky said quietly, "We prayed for a clear understanding. Don't you think this might be a very positive answer?"

"My heart wants to believe that, but my head gets in the way. I've never imagined this much debt." Ward's smile had turned to a concerned frown.

Becky's voice grew softer as she shared, "Dr. Jameson told me a number of times that worry often gives a small thing a large shadow."

Nora said as softly, "I think Shakespeare said that often in forest dark a bush becomes a bear."

Lois added, "Terry had a favorite saying too. He'd say that we should proceed, when in doubt, as though success is inevitable. I think that today there are several of us with questions about the future. Wouldn't it be wonderful if we could all be that confident?"

Steve was pretty sure that the delightful lady was thinking about his finance manager. But addressing the current question, he looked at Ward and said, "It sounds to me like your war council is saying, 'All ahead full!' We are unanimous in thinking this can only work out to your benefit. I think Nora is wise in suggesting a time period so the agreement may be examined or modified." Then as though punctuating the end of the discussion, he said, "We have that work van that could pretty easily move your boxes next week and your room is ready."

Now Ward's response was nearly a giggle. "I've decided all the furniture I have will go to Goodwill. If this reno is as classy as I think it's going to be, I had better upgrade everything." Glancing toward Becky, he said, "Maybe I can find some insightful decorating advice."

Monday morning between classes, he called Mrs. Murphy to accept her wonderful offers, with the inclusion of a time limit. She agreed that it would be a protection for them both and warned him playfully not to make major increases as their plan turned out to be a marvelous success. On Tuesday after school he moved his boxes into the Hart's garage. On Thursday Goodwill removed everything else from the house and once again tables fifteen and sixteen were filled and not selected for stand up. Apparently Florence's warning was being heeded. On Friday Phil brought the plans for approval and Ward was delighted to approve them. The project was going to be marvelous! Then he waited. The holdup was that by moving the main entrance to the east side of the building, for emergency access the house address was changed to 7600 West Greenlake Way. When the big dumpster was moved in against the back wall he knew the demolition action was about to begin.

Nora asked Ward if he had any Saturday night plans. When he assured her that he did not, she suggested that he invite "the girls" over for a casserole supper. She had an idea for the duration of the renovation. When everyone was gathered in the kitchen enjoying appetizers, she said, "We could call this date night." Her smile was mischievous. "It seems to me that we are all interested in the progress at Ward's, so we could get an update. It also seems to me that if we took turns providing the meal it would be very enjoyable for us all. Stevie could pick up the take-out dinners from P. F. Chang's just down the block from his office and I could call it in and remind him to get it on the way home. Lois could do a casserole one week, I could do the next, Becky and Sophie could share a turn, then Ward could get a couple pizzas. If my calculations are correct we could skip the Hawaii week and do two dinners each before the place is finished. What do you think?"

Everyone started to speak at once and no one was against the idea. They thanked Nora for making such a fun plan.

"It was not completely unselfish on my part," she said with that same fun smile. "I have missed Nick a whole bunch and I wonder, Honey," she grinned at Steve, "if you could invite him every so often to join us." A lovely smile blossomed on Lois even though she didn't say a word.

Ward nodded his understanding too. Then he thought of another subject. "Becky, does Sophie have a passport? I believe she'll need one for our trip. We have ten weeks, but it may take most of that to get one." Having said it, the reminder was enough to begin the process for both Sophie and Lois.

February slipped by making enormous progress. The lath and plaster walls were gone, as was all the old cupboards, wiring and plumbing. Two walls were removed from the main level and new support beams replaced them, and one more was gone from the upstairs making room for a hallway to the patio and a new bathroom for the new master bedroom. Another small bedroom was sacrificed to make walk-in closets and pocket doors so the bedrooms on either side would have access to the remodeled bathroom. Phil assured him that the project was a bit ahead of schedule and under budget because there had been no emergencies and the Home and Garden folks were delighted with it. So far there had been no surprises.

March came in like a …. Lamb. The dumpster was emptied for the final time when the crew finished removing the ceilings. In a back corner one of the workers called for Phil. He had discovered a hidden cache under the bedroom floor.

In it was a very antique dress, and a very old looking cigar box filled with old letters and some jewelry. Phil set it aside to give to Ward. He nearly forgot it because the basement slab was being poured inside the foundation. It looked much larger in real life than lines on a paper. But when Ward stopped by on his way home, Phil did remember the discovery and said it was the only mystery this old house had given up. Once again he reported that they were well ahead of schedule. Apparently the old box didn't hold a great deal of interest to him.

But when Ward told Becky about the dress and box she was very interested, or else she was using it as an excuse to invite him to bring it over so they could examine it together Carefully she unfolded the faded dress which had collected years of dust. Its pleats and lace spoke of an earlier fashion. She opened the box and began sorting the contents. A stack of letters from Eli to Billie were placed in the first pile. Two letters to Billie from Stan made the second pile and several old newspaper clippings contained photos of troops filing up gangplanks to ships. There was a gold ring, a gold locket on a chain, a string of pearls and four faded photographs. Becky softly said, "We are probably the first ones to see these pictures in seventy years." She looked closely at the young woman who was in one of the photos. "I think that's the old house in the background, but look at all the trees behind it. It looks like a forest." She studied the young couple standing in front of an old car. "I wonder who hid them so long ago."

Ward had been studying the newspaper clippings. "These are all from December of 1941 or January of 1942. I think someone was in the Army."

Becky said softly, "Would you mind if I do some sleuthing to find out more about them? This is the sort of mystery that fascinates me." Her blue eyes searched his. When he assured her that he would welcome any information about the old place, Becky admitted that she and Frieda had just been talking about how slow their jobs were at the moment. "She's just as clever at finding small tidbits of information as I am."

Ward looked closely at the locket, until he found the tiny release. "Look at these teenagers." The smiling faces of a young man and a younger woman were obviously from a much earlier time. They finally read the notes and put the story together. Eli was a young man who enlisted just after Pearl Harbor. The locket was the first gift he gave her and the pearls were the second. He asked her to protect the ring until he could properly propose. She was only sixteen and he was seventeen when he joined the Army. After a quick basic training he was shipped to Saisaih Point, Bataan in the Philippine Islands in January of '42. He wrote her a note every day. Then the two notes from Stan, who must have been Eli's buddy, told the sad story of the battle with the Imperial Japanese in April. The invaders captured both civilian and U. S. troops and marched them 60 miles to Camp O'Donnell. The first of Stan's notes informed Billie that they had been captured and he was sure that Eli had been wounded but was probably in a hospital recuperating. The second note simply shared the sad news that Eli had not survived the horrific march. As Becky read it tears ran down her cheeks. It was a seventy year old love story of sorrow.

As she sniffled back the tears, Becky was rubbing the dust from the ring. Curiously she slid it on her finger. "It fits me perfectly," she said absently. "I can only imagine the hopes and dreams it shared with Billie and how this sweet thing came to be hidden under the floor."

Frieda thought of contacting the county auditor's office for a history of owners. She learned that the original owner was Clarence Simpson, who had the home built in 1934. He was the son of the timber barren, and he had two sons and two daughters. One of the sons died in the war, the other died in '86 from heart disease. One of the daughters, Wilma Christianson, died in '97 of cancer and the other one, Charlene Walker, is living in Bay View Manor, a retirement facility in assisted living. Neither of them are named Billie. The house was sold in '54 when Clarence died of a stroke and his wife moved to California. Frieda learned that the house had seven more owners before Ward bought it.

The following Friday when Becky could see a very light schedule, she took the box to work so she could stop at Bay View on the way home. She was told that Charlene was having an exceptionally good day. She was a patient in the memory wing.

"Good afternoon, Charlene" she said cheerily. "I'm Becky. We just purchased the Green Lake house that you lived in as a girl. When we made some repairs to it, we found this old treasure box. I want to return it to you."

The wrinkled face broke into a smile. "Did you buy my old house? I really loved it there. What did you say your name is. I have trouble remembering sometimes. You know I'm soon to be 94."

Becky moved over by her and sat on the sofa. She opened the box and asked, "Were you sometimes called Billie?"

A flicker of a frown crossed the face of a woman who was trying to process the question. "No. I don't believe I ever was." Then a connection to an old memory clicked on and she added, "But my sister Wilma was called Billie once. She was three years younger than me and had a beau who wanted to marry her, but papa wouldn't hear of it. I think Billie was a secret name so papa wouldn't find out." An unfocused look peered into a vague past.

"I have found some letters Eli wrote to Billie," Becky said sweetly. When it seemed there was no interest in them, she added, "and here is a lovely old locket." That caused Charlene to brighten. When she opened it to show the senior lady, there was a bit of a gasp.

"Oh, there she is! Isn't she lovely? I always thought she was the pretty one." She held out her hand so that the locket could be more closely inspected. "Yes," the word was soft as a whisper. "Yes, there you are." A sentimental smile warmed her face.

Becky offered her the pearls and the ring, saying, "These were also in the box."

Charlene shook her head. "No thank you dear. I don't think I'll need those, you keep them. But my granddaughter will appreciate seeing her great aunt." When Becky produced the photos, Charlene said, "Oh, there you are darling. You know I always thought she was the pretty one. What did you say your name was?" The challenge of dementia was ending their brief conversation. Becky smiled knowing that her mission had been accomplished.

It was the final "date night" before the travelers left for Hawaii. Nora had prepared a wonderful roast beef dinner and topped it off with a peppermint chocolate mousse pie. When Nick offered to transport the group to the airport, Ward thanked him but assured him that the shuttle service would handle the early morning trip. "We need to be there by six thirty. It's hard to believe that we'll be in Maui for a late lunch." Once again the conversation contained several suggestions of "must see or do places".

With a huge smile Ward said, "Let me tell you about the progress on Winter Place. That's what Phil has called it and I really like it. He says the project is still on time and under budget, so much so that he has suggested a gas fireplace for the south wall of the basement as well as the one planned for the main floor family room, without hurting the budget. The exhaust vent will share an outlet on the main floor kitchen wall. The addition is framed and it contains two new commercial restrooms downstairs, The new furnace and A.C. plus two hot water heaters have been installed in the old garage area. The new garage will be large enough to park four cars but by only being two wide gives us a bunch more meeting room space." He caught his breath. "Phil is a genius," he continued. "There will be separate phone lines for upstairs, and one each for the downstairs offices. He is sure the job will be all done before Memorial day."

It was obvious that Ward was excited about the project and each person there hoped that he was aware of their reciprocal enthusiasm. When the evening drew to a close, Steve said, "You know how much we all would like to be going to Maui with you. Maybe next time we can rent a big house."

The week before spring break is usually a hectic time. Ward was glad to tally scores and see that once again all of his students were passing comfortably. He was also glad to learn that because of Jay's success with the Tootsie Roll secret, Greg Jefferson, the other algebra teacher, was using them in his class with similar results.

Thursday evening Ward agreed that instead of Giggles they should select the highlights of their trip. "We know that we can't do everything in six days," he said with a smile. "And we must save some things for our next trip there. If we make a plan, we can stick to it and not fritter away precious time there." Lois said she had always wondered about a luau. Sophie said she wanted to see the turtles. Becky said that lounging by a swimming pool would be so wonderful. Sophie said she wanted to see the turtles. She knew how to make the folks laugh. Ward shared that Nora had suggested an evening with Warren and Annabelle, which was a magic show; a visit to the aquarium. a sailboat excursion or whale watching cruise, even a ride on the narrow gauge sugar cane train could be lot of fun. They chose five highlights and agreed that gentle mornings by the pool would be ideal. Limiting their food to one major meal a day would let them fit in their clothes coming home.

The shuttle arrived ten minutes early, which caused Ward to smile and add to the gratuity. He tossed his bag in the back and directed the driver to Lois's, even though the van's GPS already knew the way. It was just such an exciting morning. In only a couple minutes he was helping with their luggage. "Everybody bring a swimsuit and their passport?" he asked playfully. "We don't need anything else." Ward was trying to ease the dreary gray of a rainy morning. He paid the driver and added a generous tip.

There was a moderate line for security but not more than they had anticipated. Breakfast was pancakes for three of them at Anthony's and finally they arrived at their boarding gate with enough time to relax. Sophie may have been the most excited. She was certainly the most talkative, with endless questions and observations. And she wanted to be right at Ward's side the whole time. Their six hour flight would be a wonderful time for her to read the new book he had brought for her, "Clarence the Stray Kitten".

Don't you just love it when the plan works? As they stepped off the plane into that warm humid air they knew they weren't in Seattle anymore. Two beautiful women wearing colorful floral dresses placed a lei on Lois, then Becky and finally on a glowing Sophie whose smile was so large it was about to burst. The fragrance of tropical flowers filled their arrival with joy., The rental car shuttle was waiting for them and the trip to the west side of the island gave them plenty of opportunity to exclaim often the warm temperature and wonders of Hawaii. When Ward stopped in Lahaina at a grocery store, he informed them that they would be back here in just four hours. The Royal Lahaina Hotel had their 6 o'clock reservation for a luau and stage production. In just a few more minutes they were in Kaanapali, where their seventh floor suite welcomed them to modern comfort and a spectacular ocean vista.

"I don't know about you guys," Ward said with a joyous smile. "But I want to get into that beautiful swimming pool. Does anyone else want to go?" There was a bit of a scramble to change clothes.

"Remember to put on some sunscreen" Becky advised. "It is still sunny enough to get a burn."

There were perhaps a half dozen folks in the large pool. When Lois selected a comfortable deck chair, Ward pulled off his tee shirt and with a couple strides, dove into the refreshing water. He swam effortlessly, thanks to the lessons Steve had provided at the Athletic Club. Becky was a bit shy when she pulled off her windbreaker robe. Ward didn't want to concentrate too long on her trim figure. But he did anyway. She sat on the side of the pool then slipped gently in. Sophie hurried to the shallow end and jumped in. She waded toward Ward but stopped when the water became chest deep. Both Ward and Becky hurried toward her to make sure this was a fun beginning for her too. Within an hour of combined effort she was splashing her way across deeper water and Ward had been brushed several times with Becky's smooth charm. That was far more refreshing than merely swimming. They finally had to get out of the pool to prepare for the evening's activities.

The busy day was finally filled to overflowing with a wonderful feast, and dancers punctuating the music of drums and guitars. Graceful women swayed as their hands told the story of the ancient days. There were whirling torches and chanting men all of which left the four feeling they had met the soul of the island. Wearily they returned to their suite. Ward had the master bedroom, which had an in suite bathroom; Lois had a room to herself and Becky and Sophie shared the third one. The ladies also shared a bathroom. It was a comfortable arrangement.

The three ladies were on the balcony looking at a star spangled sky. Ward had been busy for a moment in the kitchen until he stepped out into the darkness holding glasses of reddish fruit juice. When each of them had one, he said, "Nora told me that we should offer a toast of gratitude for the safe journey and wonderful world that God has provided for us to discover. The juice is called POG. I think it is Passion Fruit, Orange and Guava juice. For sure it is a Hawaiian specialty." He lifted his glass in a toast, saying softly, "Thank you Steve and Nora for granting us this unbelievable day." They sipped, then drank the richness of gratitude.

Lois said, "I can't remember a more enjoyable day. Come on Sophie, it's our bedtime." She kissed Ward on the cheek as she went in. Sophie gave him a sweet hug and said "I'll remember this forever." Even if she didn't, Ward was certain he would for sure.

When they were alone Becky leaned into him and added, "Ward, you are an amazing man. You have won our hearts, especially mine." Gently she leaned a bit more against him and kissed his lips, deliciously. She followed the others leaving Ward to thank whichever lucky star was up there for this perfect day.

Sunday morning they all were awake by 7 o'clock. Quietly, one by one they gathered in the living room, surprised that they were not the first one dressed. Finally Ward said, "Since I was the first one up, I get to make French Toast with heat-and-eat sausages. Is that acceptable with everyone?" The girls answered with happy nods. It was seldom that they didn't have to do the cooking.

Sophie asked, "Can we have a little more POG? I just love it." Her enthusiasm was as welcome as the warm sunshine.

When Ward served the plates, Sophie's had a candle stuck in the French Toast and they sang "Happy Birthday" to an extraordinarily delighted child. There were also several gifts wrapped in Happy Birthday paper.

Over empty glasses Ward asked, "How about this plan for the day? We'll swim for a while then drive to the aquarium. After that we'll have a late lunch at the Hula Grill in Whaler's Village where there are lots of shops if you want to get some souvenirs. When we are ready to come home we can take a swim at our beach. That should make a happy ninth birthday memory." The plan was easily accepted. Ward just hoped it would be as easily accomplished.

Ten hours later an exhausted Sophie fell asleep on the sofa. Her head comfortably snuggled on Ward's shoulder. Lois said, "That sweet child played hard today. She's wiped out and so am I. I'll see you in the morning." Looking at Ward she affectionately added, "You have made this a dream come true. I can't thank you enough, but I'll try tomorrow when I'm rested." She went to bed while Ward carried a sleeping girl into her mom's bedroom.

When he came back, Becky said, "I've still got a flicker of energy left. Would you like to take a little stroll?" They held hands as they walked to the edge of the sandy beach, then turned away from the lights into the evening shadows of the golf course. As Ward stopped, like a dancer, he guided her around in front of him so he could embrace her softness and kiss her long and sweet.

"Mmm, she whispered, "For a fellow who hadn't been kissed, you are making excellent progress." It was her turn to kiss him. "Ward, I didn't expect this trip to become romantic." He pulled her into a warmer embrace. "Now it's on my mind constantly," she whispered.

With a happy smile he said, "Your mom would tell you to behave yourself."

"Yes she would," Becky said holding on to her embrace. "But now that I am over thirty, I don't listen to her as much as I listen to my own heart." She pressed against him with growing passion and another kiss.

Ward took a ragged breath and turned them back toward the lighted building. "I can imagine that something wonderful could happen right now, but I'm not sure we would be proud of it tomorrow. Honor is not merely an idea the mind possesses; it is an idea that possesses the mind. I care so much for you that I will always let honor guide my most tender thoughts." Overhead they could see one solitary star beckoning the billions that would light the night sky.

Becky quietly chanted, "Starlight, star bright First star I see tonight, I wish I may, I wish I might, have this wish, I wish tonight." A tiny tear traced down her cheek. Her emotions were unmanageable for the moment.

Once again Ward was up and dressed before the girls. When they came out they found Granola, Yogurt and a platter of fresh Papaya on the breakfast table and a pot of tea water for anyone else who might like a cup. Of course there was ample POG too.

"We can have a lazy day today, if you want," Ward said sounding too much like a tour guide. "I thought we might have some gentle pool time, or try snorkeling over by those rocks."

There was little response or seemingly little interest. "I think we should have a light lunch," he continued bravely, "because tonight we have reservations with Warren and Annabelle the Magician." That brought a more lively response.

At the pool Ward became aware of Becky's careful distance. She wasn't avoiding him, but she was avoiding physical contact with him. At lunch she sat across from him, and at the magic show Sophie sat between them. It didn't anger him, but rather made him sad. At the expense of their enjoyment she was being careful not to repeat the warm enchantment of last night.

Wednesday morning Lois offered to scramble eggs and hoped there were still some of those heat-and-eat sausages. It was going to be another perfect day in paradise.

Ward suggested that they have only a short swim in the pool and then take the ride on the narrow gauge sugar cane train. "Then we can have a big lunch at Mama's Fish House Grill and go swimming in the Opana Point park. Yesterday I was told that there are lots of turtles there. We can either change into our swim suits there or just wear them under our shorts and shirts." Sophie squealed with anticipation.

When they arrived at Mama's however, they browsed the menu at the door and knew that they did not want to pay over two hundred dollars for lunch, "Let's go find some turtles, then go back to Hula Grill," Becky offered. "I really liked that place and all the shops around it." She was happy to know that they were already in their swimming suits.

At the park there was a rental station that offered snorkel equipment as well as foam paddle boards. "Just lay on it, paddle around and look down into the water. There are tons of fish and turtles over by the point there." He pointed to the area close to the driveway. "Just don't go out too far. There is a nasty chop today; if you get around the point it's pretty rough."

Lois said she would be quite happy watching from the shade of these palm trees. The three tested the short boards and found them very manageable and fun. Ward made sure that Sophie's ankle tether was secured so she could not let her board get away. They eased out into water a bit deeper and within a couple minutes Ward whistled and pointed in front of his board. There was a giant sea turtle! Sophie could not believe how large it was. She had forgotten that with the mask everything looks one quarter larger and one quarter closer. She slowly followed the grazing animal.

You know how quickly time flies when you are having fun. Perhaps fifteen or twenty minutes past; maybe even a bit longer slipped by under the influence of remarkable sea life. Ward had glanced at Sophie and Becky occasionally. He was confident that he was close to both, but when he looked around for them he realized that Becky was staying near the shore and Sophie was too close to the point. In fact, she was beyond it! He whistled for her, with no response. He began a more concentrated effort to get to her.

Sophie had been having trouble with her mask leaking in water. She had emptied it a couple time already and had to do it again. When she sat up, she realized how far from shore she had wandered and how bumpy the waves were becoming. She didn't see the wave approaching her, nor understand how her position on the board had tipped up the front of it. When the wave hit her board head-on, it lifted the nose of it suddenly. She leaned forward as the board, powered by a surge of water from under it, slammed into her face. Fortunately the heavy plastic lens didn't shatter causing unthinkable injury. Because the mask was in one piece, however, it concentrated the force of the blow in the area of Sophie's nose and forehead. She briefly screamed as her head snapped back from the force of the blow and she somersaulted backwards off the board! Instantly the limp child disappeared under the wave.

Ward had been watching her closely and saw the accident completely. He shouted for Becky to call 911, "Sophie needs help!"

The operator of the rental stand had heard Ward's whistle and also saw the incident. He pushed an emergency button that called for assistance and grabbed a nearby surfboard. He had more than two hundred yards to get to her.

She hadn't surfaced and Ward said, "Jesus help her!" He was stroking furiously. When he finally got to her board there was still no sign of her. He was grateful that he had attached the ankle tether. He tugged and realized he could bring her to the surface if he got into the water beside her. He released his board which would float ashore. When talking about it later he admits that he didn't have a plan. Once he saw her bloody face he knew that she was neither conscious nor breathing. He pushed the tail of her board down under her feet and as the next wave lifted, he simply pulled her to him and the floatation of the board brought her out of the water enough for him to turn her face toward him. He pinched her nose closed even though there was a lot of blood coming from it, he blew a lungful of breath mouth to mouth. The salty taste of blood was in his mouth but he did it again, and again. Then he thumped the heel of his hand against her back. No response! He did that all again, and a spout of water gushed out of her mouth. She gagged and coughed and gasped in a lungful of air. She coughed again and with a gasp said weeping, "Daddy, I'm sorry." She coughed some more but was breathing. The guy from the rental stand was almost there. Sophie's crying encouraged him to know that she was alive.

Ward had a flicker of concern about the blood in the water, He wondered if all those shark stories were founded. Nonetheless, he was trying as quickly as possible to get her back to the shore. It was difficult for him to hold her on her board with one hand and kick as hard as possible. Perhaps he had made it a quarter of the way in when a sudden burning pain ripped into his hip. His first alarmed thought was a shark attack. But there was nothing around them to suggest that. Then a second wave of pain convinced him that he couldn't continue. He tried to stroke with his one hand, which was futile. Finally help arrived. The rental guy told Ward that he could get Sophie to the beach if Ward could swim in. By the time he made it to the shore his head was spinning from the pain he was in. An aid car and two police cars were waiting for him. Standing nearby a shaken Lois held her hands to her face and a near hysterical Becky clutched a towel around a confused little girl. Ward hobbled to the aid car, grateful to be able sit down.

The EMT had done a cursory examination and determined that Sophie's nose was fractured and a deep cut on her forehead needed a couple stitches, but that was the extent of her injuries. She seemed to be breathing normally. Both she and Ward would be taken to the hospital at Kahului, right near the airport. Becky said she would follow them.

The emergency room doctor was very gentle with Sophie. After pressing the cartilage of her nose back into place, he gave her a small brace, bandaged to keep it in place. It sort of looked like one of those breath-right strips. She only whimpered a bit when she received three stitches. Then she said to her mom. "I heard Daddy Ward ask Jesus to help me and I wasn't afraid anymore."

The doctor peered at her sweet but damaged face. For clarity he asked, "Was your daddy close to you when the accident happened?" He was suspicious that he had not been given an accurate account of the incident.

"No," her small voice confessed. "I tried to follow the big turtle and I went too far into the ocean. The big wave hit me and knocked me off the floater. It was dark and scary," she took a deep breath. "Until I heard him talk with Jesus. Then they pulled me up and Jesus puffed air into me like a balloon."

The doctor's face broke into an approving smile and Becky wept as she embraced her precious daughter.

Ward had explained about the steel plate in his hip. The technician was careful as he took several X-rays. The diagnosis was good. Because of his exertion, Ward had some soft tissue damage. He had simply torn those muscles that covered his plate. With some rest they would heal just fine. Dr. Howe asked where they were staying and inquired about their return reservations. After a couple hours of observation, both patients were allowed to go home, even though Sophie's injury was turning into a gruesome bruise. The day had ushered in a dynamic new relationship for them all.

A bag of food from McDonalds' drive-through served as a welcome dinner in their wonderful room. Ward admitted that he was still pretty shaken and thought he might go down to the pool deck for a while. He needed to process that whole experience. Sophie had gone into her room to lie down. When Becky looked in on her she was sound asleep. "That kiddy sedative did the job for her," she reported. "I'll come down and join you in a while, if you don't mind."

"I will welcome you. Maybe you can help me understand what happened. It is sort of a blur right now. That was way too scary." Ward was in love with those blue eyes and the lady that studied him so affectionately.

A glorious sunset was turning the distant clouds pink and gold. He had just about decided that she wasn't going to join him when both Lois and Becky stepped out on the pool deck. They were bringing refreshments!

As Becky handed him a cold glass, she said, "This is a Mai Tai. I think the events of the day require a more adult drink than a diet coke." Her smile was happy, inviting and mysterious.

"Are you going to tell me what is in it or must I just trust you?" he asked, trying to be as humorous.

"I believe it is a rum and fruit punch. The name is Tahitian for 'good,' and you were so good today. We both think you were heroic." Becky's eyes filled with tears again,

Lois said, "Terry would have been very proud of that rescue." She raised her glass saying, "Ward, you are our hero, plain and simple, hero!" They had a sip, and then another.

Quietly Ward confessed, "When I saw it happen I didn't know what to do. I wondered if someone else would save her. Then I knew I was the only one who could. It was up to me."

He quickly took another sip because tears were forming in his eyes too.

Becky whispered, "Dr. Robert told me more than once that success often comes from not knowing our limitations. You did everything perfectly!" A tray with three more Mai Tai was brought to them. "I can't say it enough, "Thank you for what you did today." There were several more sips as she recounted the events that could have turned out tragically different. Finally, all the glasses were emptied.

They sat near the pool until the lights came on; dusk was draining the color from the sky and sea. Ward admitted that the drinks had an effect on him. He was feeling "good!" Lois said she was going to check on Sophie before turning in. She knelt beside Ward's chair and gave him a hug and then a deliberate kiss on the cheek. "You are our hero indeed!" she said.

Becky wasn't willing to end the evening yet so she asked, "Ward, are you in much pain? It looks like it is difficult for you to put much weight on that leg."

He said jokingly, "Well I'd rather talk about your cute bummy than the pain in mine." She smiled playfully knowing that without two Mai Tai he would never have uttered that sentence. He answered her question, "There's not much pain if I am still, but when I try to walk it catches my attention for sure. I hope I don't ruin the last day of our vacation. I hoped we could go back to Lahaina and explore the museum, see the old whaling ships and the famous banyan tree that was planted in the 1870's." He shrugged. "I'm afraid you guys might not go if I can't"

"Oh Ward," her voice broke with a little sob. "This trip has already surpassed every expectation I had on every level. We have seen and done so much. Please don't think you are taking away from our trip. This is such an elegant place," her voice changed to a whisper. "On top of that, I never imagined that I would ever again feel raw desire as you have awakened in me. I know I must control it, but man, have you ever lit my lights." She came over to him and softly kissed him, careful not to extend the moment too far. "May I help you get up to the room?"

He struggled to stand and then hobbled beside her with a pronounced limp.

Before they got to the elevator, she declared, "I claim the privilege of making French toast for us in the morning. I think you should rest as much as you can. Maybe we can just lounge on the pool deck and see how you and Sophie are fairing. I'll bet she will not want to be much in public with her bruised face. Maybe we could go back to the Hula Grill for supper. I can drive." He was relieved that the role of tour director had been taken by someone else.

All the rest of the plans were changed except for one. Ward had given this one too much thought and preparation to postpone. After lunch as they returned to the pool deck, he situated their little cluster by a corner away from most of the other guests. He took a deep breath and said to himself, "if you could rescue Sophie, you can do this."

He turned to Lois and said, "I have a very serious question to ask you." When she looked at him unaware of what was to follow, he asked, "Lois, may I ask for your blessing on a marriage proposal? I would very much be honored to have Becky as my wife." The other three caught their breath.

"Oh my Lord," she said delightedly. "I have never heard of a groom asking a mom for the hand of her daughter. Yes, of course I give my blessing. I would love to have you in our family." He bent down gingerly and gave her a kiss on the cheek.

Turning to Sophie he asked, "My charming mermaid, may I ask your mom to be my wife, making me your dad?" He was pretty sure her heart was pounding with approval.

"Yes, yes, oh yes," she squealed. "Does this mean you get to live in our house?" Her innocent joy was delightful.

Ward nodded and answered her, "Yup! Something like that. We might need to find a larger place with another bathroom, but we will all be together."

"Yes, yes, yes! I've forever wanted a daddy. This is wonderful!" Not even her bruised face could dampen her joy. Ward bent down and gently kissed her cheek too.

He eased himself down on his good knee. "Becky, love, I apologize if I have already polled the jury without your permission. I so want to spend our forever together." He offered her a precious diamond ring. "Will you consider becoming my bride? Will you marry me?" Now his heart was pounding with anticipation. Folks on the other side of the pool were applauding.

Becky knelt in front of him and answered, "More than I can ever express to you I will be delighted to marry you. Ward you are my dream come true!" She kissed him eagerly and the applause doubled. She looked at her dazzling ring and asked, "How did you know my size. This is just perfect. She waved her hand so the others across the pool could see.

"When you tried on the gold band from the hidden box, you said it was perfect. I just took it in to Goldfarb's and asked them to make yours the same size. He pulled her to him for another kiss. In a confidential voice he said to Sophie, "I hear that the Hula Grill has the best celebration chocolate sundaes in the world. Shall we go see?"

The rental car was returned and the shuttle took them back to the departure gate. As Ward hobbled to the check-in desk, he was greeted with a wide smile. "I'll bet you are the Winter party," the lady said. "Dr. Howe told us to treat you gently." She looked at Sophie and asked, "Is this the little lady who nearly became a mermaid?" When she shyly nodded the lady confirmed, "You heard your daddy praying for you, huh?" Another slight nod. "Dr. Howe is one of finest men of faith and medicine on the island. You touched his heart with your courage. He was delighted to upgrade you to first class for your comfort on the way home." Becky gave Sophie a happy hug. When their bags were checked in, and their boarding passes printed, a man pushing a wheelchair for Ward and a lady carrying three white Plumeria leis, approached and presented a lovely Hawaiian farewell. "Aloha," they said. "Please come back to visit us again soon." They were escorted through security and boarded before any other passengers.

Ward said softly to Becky, "This doesn't take away the hurt, but doesn't it make you feel like a celebrity?"

"There are layers of emotions aren't there?" Becky asked in the same soft voice. "I'm sad to go but delighted with the experience. I'm looking forward to what's ahead but already missing this place. Do you suppose we'll come back?"

"I'm counting on it," Ward said with a happy grin. "Perhaps we could honeymoon here and take care of some unfinished business."

"Wouldn't that be nice?" she answered with a sigh. Becky had been watching the folks boarding behind them. Suddenly she raised her hand and said, "Dr. Strong? Hello." The man looked casually toward her and Becky added, "I'm Becky Stanley, from your UW Political Science class."

The prominent looking man chuckled and said, "Oh my, that goes back a ways. It's been twelve or fourteen years. You know I'm not at the U anymore. I'm in Olympia, in charge of the state board of education." He was aware of the line behind him so he casually said, "It's nice of you to remember old times. I hope we see one another again." It was a forecast that was sure to happen.

It was almost 4 o'clock before Ward arrived back with Steve and Nora. They were alarmed to hear about the near tragedy with Sophie, but delighted to hear that the proposal went so well. Immediately Nora got up to call Lois, even though they would just be walking through the door. When she finally connected she offered a date night dinner. "Your frig is probably empty," she said with a chuckle. "And you're too bushed to go to the store. Come on over. You don't have to stay long. We just want to see your tan faces and the lovely ring on Becky's hand." She didn't mention Sophie's bruised face. She didn't tell her that Nick was already there.

During the meal, highlights of the Hawaii trip were shared. Sophie recalled the fun of the magic show. "The man lit a big firecracker, but when it went off instead of a big bang, a feather flower appeared, just for me because it was my birthday. He borrowed money from a man in the front row. Did you know that each bill has its own number? Then, right at the last, he took a lemon from a lady who had been holding it for most of the show as part of another trick. When the lemon was cut in two, the man's same number money was inside of it." She giggled, "I know it was a trick, but he sure fooled me."

Lois explained that the first night the hotel had a luau. "The food was wonderful, but the hula dancing was unforgettable. The men with the torches were amazing too. I was afraid everything after that would be secondary. It just set the tone of wonderful for the whole week."

Becky said quietly, "Your accommodations were so splendid. I was looking forward to lounging by the pool. When Ward asked my mom if she would bless a marriage proposal, that pool deck became so much more. I'll never forget the thrill of that day."

Sophie spoke in an ever softer voice, "I'll never forget the turtles. I was so interested I forgot the warning we had been given. I watched him eat as he went into the deeper water. That's where the big wave banged the board into my face. I heard Daddy Ward ask Jesus to help me, and he did." She looked at Ward and the others at the table felt the adoration. "The doctor at the hospital said I was a lucky girl to know Jesus. I didn't tell him that I was a lucky girl to have a Daddy Ward too."

"I'm the lucky one," Ward said in the same soft voice. "Steve, your generosity with the condo, was magnificent. Then in that terrible scary moment I became aware of the bonds of love we have." He glanced around the table. "She said 'yes'! That was the most amazing moment for me." He visibly relaxed and a happy smile bloomed on his face. The conversation ended with the agreement that there was a lot of highlights awaiting their next trip. Both Lois and Nick nodded agreement as they held hands.

Lois said, "It was wonderful to see some of the island. Tonight I am grateful to be home. I had almost forgotten that tomorrow is Palm Sunday. Would you like to celebrate Easter with us next Sunday? Afterward, we could have a Salmon House brunch." Nick gave her hand a happy squeeze. He was very grateful they were home too.

Nora asked, hoping that she was not preying, "Have you thought about a wedding date?"

Becky answered before Ward, "We're still in the wonder of the joy of the prospect. We have talked about a church wedding, or the fist one on the patio. I think we both are eager, but also willing to make sure we have some wise counsel." She gave a characteristic shrug and a happy smile.

Ward added, "We don't want to make plans that would interfere with Jay and Florence's. What do you guys think about it?"

Nora started to answer but Sophie said, "If you are married before school is out, we can play together all summer." Her smile, even from a bruised face, was big and bright.

Nora said finally, "I was about to suggest that we help you pray for the increase of knowing what is best for your hearts, Remember it's a journey, not a destination."

Nick looked fondly at Lois and said softly, "You are going to be pretty lonesome after having these delightful ladies so long. Perhaps date night suppers might continue, even after the wedding." It was the first time he had suggested a future plan.

Monday morning Ward was still limping obviously. Jay pulled into the faculty parking right behind Ward. As he walked in with him he asked, "How in the world did you hurt yourself in Hawaii? I thought that was sandy beaches and cool drinks." His warm smile suggested a genuine caring.

"Well it wasn't all leisure," Ward replied. "I wiped out on the North Shore curl. That will teach me for trying to keep up with the locals." It was a fabrication that grew during the next several telling. It masked the memory of a dreadful moment that still caused him to shiver.

Thursday night there were three missing from tables fifteen and sixteen. Sam, Maria and Caroline chose to attend services in their church. Lou continued to skip over the stand up selections so there was ample opportunity for conversations and planning for the spring and summer. Just at the conclusion of the open mic, a serving person presented a bottle of champagne to table sixteen and the overhead selection light drew the attention of the crowd. Jay had planned his moment well.

He knelt before Florence, offering to hold her hand. "Florence, Sweetheart, you are the highlight of every day, every hour. I can only imagine how wonderful a life with you will be. Will you be my bride? Will you marry me and become the highlight of the rest of my life?" A single tear traced down his cheek.

In a heartbeat she knelt with him saying, "Oh yes, I am so honored and delighted to be your bride. Giggles may lose us to happy ever after." She leaned into him for a tender kiss, and a spirited applause; even Lou joined in with a big grin.

The champagne was opened and eagerly shared by the happy crowd. When Florence looked at Ward and said, "You are a wonderful totem! I'm not sure any of this would have happened without you." The laughter was an approving blessing. "I do hope we can get on your calendar for the sky patio. Nothing could be more perfect."

Well, maybe Easter morning might have been a perfect candidate. A sunny April morning with tulips and daffodils blooming and the Presbyterian church was filled with happy worshipers. Ward could sense the joyous atmosphere as he entered the church again. There were folks stationed at every door to welcome each one. Lois had a big smile from the moment she walked in. She was going to fill an entire pew with her people. Nick sat beside her then, Steve and Nora, then Becky, Sophie and Ward. She hadn't been this happy in church for a long time.

It seemed to Ward that there was a lot of chatting going on around him, until the organist began softly playing Beethoven's "*Joyful, Joyful*". The music swelled and the chatting quieted. A choir director stood and invited the congregation to stand and sing the words as the mighty organ gained more depth and power. As the people sang the choir filed in by the center aisle. Just like that, Ward thought, "That's not fair! We've only begun and I am already thrilled!" There was inspiration all around him, especially when he could clearly hear Sophie and Becky singing.

A worship leader welcomed the full house and invited everyone to greet those around them. Ward was warmly greeted by those in front and behind him. When Sophie reached to hug him she was careful not to rub the make-up her mom had applied to hide the green remnant of her bruised face. Her joyous smile was even better than a hug. A prayer was shared and then a young man and woman sang a Larnell Harris song, "*I've Just Seen Jesus.*" The power of inspiration grew stronger. A prayer was spoken addressing current petitions and needs, the Bible reading was from Luke 24, verses 1 through 8 and the choir sang a moving rendition of "*He Lives.*" Finally, Pastor Shannon stood for the morning homily.

"Good morning. Do you have childhood memories around Easter? Some may only be about colored eggs or dinner with grandma. Others may be about new clothes. My earliest association about Easter was about death, not resurrection. It stemmed from a horrible memory from one sunny Easter Sunday and the only cat I ever owned. Boots was a six week old kitten, solid black except for white "boots" on each foot, as if she had daintily stepped in a tray of white paint. She lived in a cardboard box on our back porch and slept on a pillow stuffed with cedar shavings. My mother, insisting that Boots must learn to defend herself before sampling the huge outdoors, had set the trial date of Easter. Boot's big test.

"At last the day arrived. Georgia sunshine had already coaxed spring into full bloom. Boots sniffed the grass and batted a daffodil. She stalked a butterfly, leaping as high as she could and missing. She kept us joyously entertained until the neighbor's kids came over for an Easter egg hunt.

"When our playmates arrived the unthinkable happened. Their pet Boston Terrier, Pugs, followed them into our yard, spied Boots, let out a low growl, and charged. We all screamed and ran to defend the kitten, but Pugs was quicker and had Boots in its mouth, shaking it like a toy. We helplessly watched the flashing teeth and tuffs of fur. Finally Pugs dropped the limp kitten and trotted off.

"I could not have articulated it at the time, but what I learned that Easter under the noonday sun was the ugly word *irreversible*. All afternoon I prayed for a miracle. "No, it can't be! Tell me it's not true. Maybe Boots will come back." I reasoned that our Sunday school teacher had told us such a story about Jesus. Maybe the whole tragic afternoon could just be erased, deleted. We could keep Boots safe on the porch forever. A thousand schemes ran through my nine year old mind until reality won. I accepted at last the fact that Boots was irreversibly dead.

"From then on, Easter Sundays in my childhood were stained by the memory of the death in the grass. As the years increased, I would learn more about the word irreversible. My final year in seminary was marked by the loss of three good friends. Leonard, a young man who was a faithful usher and businessman left a working lunch at a restaurant. Somewhere between the door and the parking lot, his heart stopped. Another was Gretchen, a school teacher who took a year off to serve as a mission nurse in Guatemala. A fire trapped her in the dormitory where she was staying. She and three other nurses could not escape and lost their lives. A third, Bob a fellow seminarian, died scuba diving at the bottom of Lake Michigan. Life came unexpectedly to a halt that year. I spoke at all three funerals, and each time as I struggled with what to say the old ugly word irreversible came flooding back, with greater force than I can describe. Nothing I could say, nothing I could do would accomplish what I wanted above all else: to have my friends back.

"On the day Bob made his final dive I was sitting oblivious in the student library of the University of Chicago. I was reading an assignment: My Quest for Beauty by Rollo May. In his book the famous therapist recalls a scene from his lifelong search for beauty, especially a visit to Mt. Athos, a peninsula of monasteries attached to Greece. There he stumbled upon an all-night celebration of Greek Orthodox Easter. Incense hung heavy in the air. The only light was from a multitude of candles. At the climax of that service, the priest gave everyone three Easter eggs, splendidly decorated and wrapped on a veil. "Christos Anesti!" he said – "Christ is Risen!" Each person present, including Rollo May, replied according to custom, "He is risen indeed!"

"Rollo May writes: "I was seized then by a moment of spiritual reality: What would it mean for our world if He had truly risen?" I read that Passage just before returning home to learn that Bob had died. Rollo May's question floating around in my mind, hauntingly, after I heard the terrible news. What did it mean for our world that Christ had risen?

"In the cloud of grief over Bob's death, I began to see the meaning of Easter in a new light. As a nine-year-old on Easter Sunday I had learned the harsh lesson of irreversibility. Now as an adult, I saw that Easter actually held out the awesome promise of reversibility. Nothing, not even death, was final. Even that could be reversed!

"When I spoke at Bob's funeral, I rephrased Rollo May's question in terms of our particular grief. What would it mean for us if Bob rose again? We were sitting in a chapel, numbed by three days of mourning, death bearing down on us like a crushing weight. How would it be to walk out into the parking lot and there to our utter astonishment, find Bob? Bob! With his bounding stride, his crooked grin, his clear gray eyes? It could be no one else but Bob, alive again!

"The image gave us a hint of what the disciples of Jesus felt on the first Easter. They too had grieved three days. On Sunday they heard the bell-like clarion announcement. Easter hits a new note of hope and faith that what God did once in a graveyard in Jerusalem, he can and will do again on grand scale. For Bob, for us, for the world, against all odds, the irreversible will be reversed!

"We who read the gospels from the other side of Easter, forget how difficult it must have been for the disciples to process that event. In itself the empty tomb did not convince them. That fact only demonstrated that "He is not Here," not "He is risen." Convincing those skeptics would require intimate, personal encounters with the one who had been their Lord for three years. Over six weeks Jesus provided just that.

"Author Frederick Buechner is struck by the mundane manner of Jesus risen appearances. There were no angels in the sky singing choruses, no trumpet sounds, nor kings from far off bearing gifts. Jesus showed up in the most ordinary circumstance: a private dinner, two men walking a discouraged road home, a woman weeping in the garden, some fishermen working on a lake. The appearances are not spectacular, but flesh-and-blood encounters. Jesus can always prove his identity. No other living person has ever born the scars of crucifixion. Still, the disciples fail to recognize him right away. Painstakingly he condescends to meet the level of the skepticism. For suspicious Thomas it means a personal invitation to touch his wounds that Thomas may believe. For the humiliated Simon Peter, it means a bittersweet scene of reconciliation and forgiveness.

"The appearances, as many as a dozen, show a definite pattern. Jesus visited small groups of people in a remote area or closed indoors. Although these private encounters bolstered the faith of those who already believed in Jesus, as far as we know not a single unbeliever saw Jesus after his death. Why limit visitations to just his friends? Why not reappear on Pilate's porch, or before the Sanhedrin, this time with a withering burst of holy justice? Perhaps a clue of his strategy can be found in his words to Thomas: 'Because you have seen me, you have believed; blessed are those who have not seen and yet have believed.'

"Think about that for a minute. The blessing given to the disciples is offered to you and to me as well! Except for a limited few people to whom the resurrected Jesus appeared, every Christian who has ever lived falls into the category of "blessed." I ask myself, "Why do I believe? – I who may resemble Thomas more than any other disciple in my skepticism and slowness to accept what cannot be proven beyond a doubt.

"In your worship folder I put seven excerpts from Frank Morison's book, "Who Moved the Stone?" Although Morison set out to discount the resurrection as a myth, the evidence he read convinced him otherwise. Faith requires the possibility of rejection, or it's not faith. So again I ask, "What then gives me Easter faith?"

"One reason I am open to belief, I admit, is that at a very deep level I want the Easter story to be true. Faith grows out of a subsoil of yearning, and some primal cry rejects the reign of death. We humans resist the idea of death having the final word. We want to believe otherwise.

"I remember the year I lost my three friends. Above all else, I want Easter to be true because of its promise that someday I'll be reunited with them. I want to abolish the word irreversible forever.

"On a more primary level, I believe in Easter because I have gotten to know God. I know that God is Love and I also know that we human beings want to keep alive those whom we love. I do not let my friends die; they live in my memories and my heart long after I can no longer see them. They live in me through all the wonderful lessons they have given me. For whatever reason – human freedom lies at the core, I imagine – God allows a planet where a man dies scuba diving in the prime of his life and a woman dies in a tragic fire. But I believe – if I did not believe this, I would not believe in a loving God - that God is not satisfied with such a blighted planet. Divine love has a way to overcome. Jon Donne wrote, 'Death be not proud; God will not let death win.' Believing in Easter entails believing in a loving God.

"One important detail in the Easter story has always intrigued me. Why did Jesus keep the scars from his crucifixion? Don't you imagine he could have had any resurrected body he wanted? Yet he chose to keep the scars of the nails and spear that could be seen and touched. Why?

"I believe the story of Easter would be incomplete without those scars on the hands, the feet, the side of Jesus. When humans fantasize, we dream of a perfect body having lean muscles, straight pearly teeth and a lush head of curly hair. We know that is an unnatural state, the perfect body. But for Jesus being confined in a human skin was the unnatural state. The scars are to him a permanent reminder of the days of suffering and sacrifice.

"I take hope in Jesus' scars. They represent the most horrible event that has ever been inflicted. Even that event, though - the crucifixion – Easter turned into a memory of love. Because of Easter, I can hope that the tears we shed, the blows we receive, the emotional wounds, the heartache over lost friends and loved ones, all these will become memories like Jesus' scars. Scars never go away, but neither do they hurt any longer. We will have re-created bodies, an Easter body. We will have a new start – an Easter start. When I take Easter as the starting point I see how God treats those he loves and Easter is seen as a preview of ultimate reality. Hope then floats like lava under the crust of daily life."

"Let me conclude this morning with a story I first heard from Dr. Leslie Weatherhead. It requires some imagination on your part because it is a conversation between a Voice and an unborn baby. The Voice says to the baby, Are you ready?"

"The baby answers, "Ready for what?"

"The Voice replies, "Ready to leave this place, to be on your own, to grow and learn and love."

"Did you say, 'leave this place,' the babe asks in shock. "No, I can't leave. Mom feeds me, comforts me. She cares for me and even sings, which fills my whole world with music. No! I couldn't possibly leave this place."

"But in the fullness of time that babe was born and his first experience was that of tender arms welcoming him and careful hands ministering to his need. The baby grew, and learned and discovered wonders upon wonders. He travelled, learned, knew love. Then one day, quite by surprise, the Voice returned and asked, "Babe, are you ready?"

"The mystified babe answered, "Ready for what?"

"Gently the Voice said, "To be born into a vast mystery of eternal freedom; to leave this place and enter a much larger experience, where you will know pure peace, joy and love."

"Wait," the babe protested. Did you say leave this place? I just cannot do that. I have tasks to complete, children to raise, conversations to finish. I have a life to live."

"But we know that in a blink he was gone.

"Easter brings us a question about the nature of God who knows no irreversibility. Brokenness is mended, guilt is forgiven, sin is overcome, division is unified and death is defeated once and for all. The babe's first experience is that of warm welcome and tender care. That is our Easter faith."

Pastor Shannon smiled and asked, "Why do we believe in Easter?' The organist played a familiar melody which the choir had used to begin the service. "Sing with me," the pastor invited.

"I serve a risen Savior, he's in the world today;" Some of the congregation began to sing with her.

"I know that he is living, whatever foes may say." The volume of voices increased.

"I see his hand of mercy, I hear his voice of cheer," The folks seated at the front stood to sing and the congregation followed their lead.

"and just the time I need him, he's always near." Full volume the folks matched the organ's power.

"He lives, he lives, Christ Jesus lives today! He walks with me and talks with me along life's narrow way. He lives, he lives, salvation to impart! You ask me how I know he lives? He lives within my heart." They sang together the concluding two verses.

"Bow with me in prayer," the pastor invited. "Gracious generous Lord God, in the glory of this morning, we ask that you grant us the certainty that beyond death there is life, where the broken things are mended and the lost things found; where there is rest for the weary and joy for the sad; where all we have hoped and willed for good shall exist, where the dream will come true and the ideal will be realized, where we shall be forever with our Lord. So grant us the Easter certainty that life is stronger than death through Jesus Christ our Risen Lord. Amen."

The conclusion of the worship service was music from the organ and choir. There was also much drying of eyes for those who had found her words inspiring. While it was not spoken at the moment, there was a unanimous agreement among Lois' pew that they would be happy if this could become a frequent experience.

Ward's second period class was interrupted by a request from the office to bring Ted Lawson and Paul Brock to Mr. Reese's office immediately. Ward looked at Ginger Jameson and asked if she wanted to toss Tootsie Rolls for him. When she smiled and nodded, he invited the two fellows to accompany him. As they walked down the empty hall they assured him they had no idea what the cause of this might be.

The secretary gestured to Mr. Reese's office and told Ward to go right in. The others were already there. As Ward opened the door, he was surprised to see Harry Sherman and Bob Bagley, also outstanding members of the basketball team and they were accompanied by their fathers. A stern faced Seattle police officer was also with them.

"Thank you, Mr. Winter. You may return to your class." There was a smugness that warned Ward that this might be sinister.

"What's going on here," the teacher asked. "Is there some problem."

With a snarl, the principal said, "Return to your class Mr. Winter. This is none of your business."

Ward closed the door without leaving the room. Quietly he said, "These are my students, that makes it my business."

"Be careful, sir," Mr. Reese snarled. "You were on probation when you came to us a couple years ago and you are very close to being there again." He stood up and said triumphantly, "These troublemakers were seen vandalizing our offices last night. They are being charged with trespassing and destruction of property. Didn't you see the mess on the front of our school this morning? They insulted this school and me with the outline of a rooster!" Both Paul and Ted shook their heads in disbelief and denial.

"Who saw them do that?" the confused teacher asked. He knew there was something very wrong going on.

"I said this is none of your business!" Mr. Reese nearly shouted. "But I will tell you that as the Area Directors meeting was breaking up we saw them run for their car and drive away. I'm not the only one who recognized them." He was becoming too defensive.

One of the dads said to Ward, recognizing him now as an ally, "We've tried to explain to Mr. Reese that our boys were home all evening. They never left the house."

Ward was trying to process all this and noticed that the police officer shook his head and looked at his feet. "What time did you say you saw them do this?" he asked with a puzzled expression.

The principal hissed, "I said it was none of your business. But to satisfy your prying question, we saw them at nine fifteen or nine twenty. There was no mistake!" Mr. Reese's face was blushing from the anger he was feeling.

Quietly Ward said, "Sir, respectfully I don't know how that could have been the case. Paul and Ted were with me last night, watching the video, 'Stand and Deliver'. It is a requirement in our teaching plan. They missed it because of the snow days and were trying to make up the omission. They still have a quiz to complete the assignment." He shrugged as the two young men realized what it means for another to "have your back." Their expressions did not indicate anything but submissive attention.

Now the principal's face turned white with fury. "Winter, that may have cost you your job!"

Ward couldn't look at him without showing disrespect so he looked at the floor. In a voice just above a whisper he said, "Perhaps, sir. It wouldn't be the first time. Maybe one of us will soon be selling cars again."

The officer stood up and said to the boys and their dads, "The custodians have washed the evidence away and there is no credible witnesses so there is no reason we should continue this. You are free to go. Thank you for your patience." He walked out of the room without looking at either Mr. Reese or Ward.

At lunch the irritation grew for Mr. Reese, when he heard someone ask to purchase a 'Rooster Bar' from the Decca shelf.

He walked over to the counter and asked angrily, "What did you just say to me?"

There were a half dozen confused faces that turned toward him. The young teacher who was managing the Decca sales answered, "I'm sorry, Mr. Reese, did you ask for something?"

"Don't get cute with me." He looked at the image of a rooster scribbled on the chalk board on the far wall. "I heard someone ask for a Rooster Bar."

She was embarrassed by the accusation and suddenly felt like she was speaking to a child. "Sir we have these Booster Bars," she said very clearly. I didn't hear anyone ask for anything different."

"If you don't change the name, we'll need to discontinue them," he said finally realizing how ridiculous he was sounding. "Where do they come from anyway?"

The young woman answered, "There are three young moms who are trying to start their bakery business. They make enough each day for three high schools, we being one, to have six trays each. We sell out every day."

"What are they made of? Have the ingredients been approved by our dietitian?" He was still riled from the interference he had experienced in his office.

"Sir they are excellent nutrition for the students. They are made only with oatmeal, milk, honey and powdered sugar. That's why we call them 'Booster Bars'. We sell out of them ever day, raising about $150 each day for our Decca program."

As he turned and sulked away, he growled. "Change the name or you won't be selling them here anymore."

Someone outside in the hall crowed, "Cock-a-doodle-do!". Mr. Reese knew that he had lost another battle.

Before school was out for the afternoon the account had spread like wildfire: "Mr. Winter has your back!" And almost every chalk boards began to show an outline of a rooster with the name J. J. Reester!

Not surprising by the next morning all Roosevelt teachers had a memo in their mailbox from J. J. Reese, Principal, which said: "Starting immediately no food may be distributed to students by teachers, no cupcakes cookies or bits of candy." He may have lost battles but he wanted them to know he had not lost the war, yet.

Ted Lawson's dad wrote a letter to Dr. Bradley Anthony, the Seattle Superintendent, admitting that he had painted the white letters on the school window and the image of a rooster. He was careful to avoid any lasting damage but had to express his anger at a faculty leader who was so uncaring and completely oblivious to the lasting damage he was willing to inflict on the Roosevelt students. The letter also praised a teacher who was willing to do just the opposite of that for his students. The letter concluded, "My son learned the lesson of courage yesterday by a teacher who was willing to give up his job to prevent such a travesty. We need more like him!"

Thursday morning Ward's week was back to normal, finally. He was eager to see Becky and Sophie. He was even thinking about returning to Giggles. The very last person he expected to interrupt his second period class was the principal. Yet when the door opened there he was. He stepped in the classroom like a conquering general; he looked first at the image of a rooster on the chalkboard, then at the sack of Tootsie Rolls on the teacher's desk.

"Mr. Winter you were explicitly instructed not to distribute food to your students. It doesn't surprise me that your insubordination has chosen to disregard those instructions and draw such an insult on your board." Ward had no idea who was doing the artwork in nearly every room. "Please take your things," he brushed the bag of candy into the wastepaper basket, "and leave the building. You are suspended until we can find a solution to this." Defiantly, he crossed his arms over his chest.

"Yes sir," Ward said submissively. He picked up his briefcase from under the desk, pulled a couple books out of the desk drawer and put on his jacket. Very deliberately he bent and retrieved the sack of Tootsie Rolls. He smiled and delivered it to Ginger saying with a wink, "Give these to some hungry souls." Just that simply, he walked out of the door.

Several seconds of stunned silence passed before the principal said, "Well now, where are we?" He opened the algebra textbook.

Ginger had a mischievous smile as she stood and folded her notebook. She looked at her fellow students and picked up her jacket. With a shrug she quietly asked, "Anybody want to stay for the rest of this silliness?" Every other student in the room rose to leave.

"Wait just a moment," the principal ordered. "You don't have my permission to go."

Silently the entire class walked out. He had just lost the war!

Ginger went into Jay Taylor's classroom and quietly shared what had just occurred. She invited them to join her in a silent walk-out. Few had to be asked twice. Paul Brock interrupted Greg Jefferson's class with the same invitation. The three classes of students left the building without saying a word.

And then, OMG! Facebook exploded with the whole story about a disgruntled administrator and a courageous teacher. Pictures of the students sitting on the steps of the school eating Tootsie Rolls were posted and went viral instantly. Jay emailed Florence who forwarded the message to Becky; Greg emailed Frieda who forwarded the message to Becky. Becky forwarded the message to the superintendent and Frieda forwarded the message to the teacher's union office. Within minutes three TV stations had people on the way to cover the Tootsie Roll walk-out. Becky was about to leave her office to find Ward, but before she did, she sent another email to Frieda: "Will you please look into the background of Reese. This sounds pretty unstable to me. Has he had any evidence of this in his past?"

Ward's first stop was the reno project. The new windows were being installed and the roofers were finishing the new extension. Phil told him that the patio would be roughed in by Saturday. "This is becoming a fascinating project," he said proudly. "Next week we will have the siding on and the painters will give her a light green finish." Ward took a quick walk-through, more impressed than ever. He could now envision the upstairs changes. If nothing else, these moments in the exciting new structure softened the bitterness he was feeling about the high school principal who was so out of control. "He's worse than I ever thought of being in Spokane," he mused.

Then he went home, not sure what he would say to Nora. The finality of the suspension was beginning to set in. He definitely needed to talk with her and Steve.

Like a perfect mom, before he could begin to give her a report of the series of events, she placed a cup of tea in front of him saying, "I believe Earl Grey has a calming effect." He had not opened his computer to learn what an avalanche of texts were filling his in-box. By noon over four hundred had arrived and over a hundred emails.

Becky arrived a few minutes later. Her smile was always welcome, but this moment seemed to make it much more so. "Sweetie, you are probably not aware what has happened at school in the last two hours. When the second period let out most of the rest of the school heard what had happened."

Ward interrupted her, "Wait, what happened?"

"Sorry, you couldn't have known because you left," Becky apologized. "Ginger Jameson was only a couple minutes behind you. She asked the rest of the class to follow her in a silent protest."

With a shocked smile Ward asked, "What?"

Becky continued, "Yes, she went to both the other algebra classes and invited them to join. When the second period bell rang, nearly half the student body joined in the protest on the front steps. I heard it was eerie quiet. They sat on the steps eating Tootsie Rolls. All three channels had film crews recording a most unusual sight."

"Oh man," Ward groaned, "I sure hope they don't get crossways with Reese. That is the most irritating man I know. I'd feel rotten if I started something that they are going to pay for."

Becky placed her hand on his saying, "I don't think anyone knows how this day is going to turn out. But I'm pretty sure that neither you nor the students are going to be in trouble. My feeling is that Mr. Reese will bear the burden. Let's turn on the noon news and see if you are on the front page." All afternoon she stayed with Ward, answering emails and occasionally phone calls, none of them negative.

She was just getting ready to go home when the phone rang yet again. Playfully she had been answering, "Mr.

Winter's office, May I take a message?" The lady on the other end of the conversation said simply, "Superintendent Brad Anthony would like to speak with Mr. Winter at his earliest convenience."

In an apologetic voice Becky said, "He is right here. I'll put him on."

"Mr. Winter, I'm Brad Anthony, Superintendent of the Seattle School District. You and I haven't met, but I'm pretty sure that is about to change. Have you been following the news from Roosevelt this afternoon?"

"No sir," Ward replied. "Only a few emails and texts."

"I believe the evening news will be of some interest to you. I've known a lot of popular teachers before, but none who have been teaching less than a full year and who have an army of supporters as you do. I might start calling them Ward's Warriors, like Arny's Army. I haven't seen this much energetic action since the civil rights marches of the 60's. I'm not sure if the students are praising you or bringing an autocratic problem to our attention. Maybe it's a bit of both. The reason for this call is to assure you that your teaching contract is in order and I expect you to be in class tomorrow morning. Mr. Reese had no authority to place you on suspension. We are looking into the matter. I may need to get your statement later, but for today I need you back in class. Do you have any questions about that?"

"None sir," Ward responded. "Thank you for clearing that up for me."

The evening news was amazing. The cameras captured a crowd of nearly three hundred students sitting or standing near the main stairway into the school. There were no noisy demands being made only silence or at least very quiet conversations.

"It seems," the announcer said in an equally subdued voice, "that the students are in a silent protest over the suspension of a popular teacher. The teacher is accused of rewarding his students who have a correct test with a small Tootsie Roll.

Yes, you heard that correctly. In light of the all-too-common tragic violence we have recently witnessed, or the shocking allegations of misconduct, this one is refreshing and a real human interest story. I'd like to meet that teacher."

At the bell ending the third period, the demonstration broke up, just as quietly as it started. Some of the students had no idea what the issue had been, some were just happy to be able to skip a class and some were just hungry for lunch. But there were about sixty algebra students who felt the satisfaction of standing for a principle, even if it was only as small as a Tootsie Roll. Ginger Jameson, however realized a hidden desire within her. She wanted to become more involved in social action and the protection of the marginalized.

The next morning second period students found a Tootsie Roll on their desk. When the bell rang and folks were settled Ward thanked them. "One of my favorite truisms says, 'To see what is wrong and correct it, is the soul of courage, and to see what is right and not do it, is the failure of courage.' I couldn't be more honored by your courage on my behalf. Did you watch the evening news?" There were several comments about the incident.

Before he turned their attention to the workbook, Ginger said softly, "If our leader stands for what is clearly right, courage is not so demanding, and when we stand together our courage is bonded strength. Yesterday was about you, but not only you. Mr. Reese has been an embarrassment frequently. You just gave us a perfect opportunity to do what many of us have wished for. Thank you."

Ted Lawson in the back of the room began an applause that was instantly joined by all the students.

Finally, Ward said, "O.K. that's enough sentiment. We have some work to do. Now how many of you did the exercise?" All hands were raised. "O.K. Now how many have these answers that I have written on the board?" Again all hands were raised. "You are making my job so easy. Enjoy a Tootsie Roll and use the rest of the hour doing your other homework. You folks are radically fine." Apparently there was still a bit of time for sentiment and he had just developed a casual model that would serve the rest of the school year.

Wednesday afternoon Ward took a phone call in the faculty room.

"Mr. Winter, this is the office of Bradley Anthony, the Seattle Superintendent of Schools. I would like to schedule a conference that will meet your mutual availabilities. What is your final afternoon class?"

"I have a fourth period class that ends at 1:40 every afternoon." Ward's anxiety was pretty high, even though the superintendent had assured him that his contract was solid.

"Oh, that is most workable," her happy voice responded. "Tuesday afternoons are usually pretty quiet right now. Can you be here next Tuesday, May twelfth by about 2:15? We can schedule other meetings after that if necessary. I'll schedule this with Dr. Anthony and see you next Tuesday. Thank you for your cooperation."

Ward was left wondering what the heck might be cooking this time.

Thursday evening Giggles tables fifteen and sixteen were full again and seating seemed to by couples. Sam and Maria were happy to join Jay and Florence, Ward and Becky. Much of the conversation focused on the student demonstration and the positive TV coverage. Florence shook her head at Lou when he asked if she had a stand up. Then much of the conversation focused on Ward's renovation project and the possibility of a wedding on the sky patio.

Ward's grin was almost boyish. "You can't believe how easy it was to get on the Marriage Clerk's list. An attorney's recommendation, thirty five dollars and about an hour of training. The law requires that you must have two witnesses, preferably sober ones, then, in front of them, you must promise to" he held up one finger, "live together" he held up another finger, "as wife and husband. Then I have a month to return the signed documents. Cinchy. The charm is added by personal touches, music or readings. I doubt if it will happen often, but I think that will be a hoot."

Sam asked, "Will you rent out the space for other groups?"

"I haven't gone that far in the discussion. But I'm going to be very selective for a while, after all this will be my home. The idea of a marriage mill is pretty disgusting to me. I think I told you that the Republican's are going to be there at least a couple times a week. We'll see how much volume that brings"

Florence suggested, "It would be enjoyable if we could switch this group over on Thursday night, especially in the summer when we could stay a little longer than eight o'clock. Maybe we could order in some Pizza occasionally." Ward winked at Becky. There were a ton of possibilities.

Friday night Ward and Becky had a dinner for two at Ivar's Salmon House. It was an unusually quiet evening on Lake Union with only a handful of boats and a horde of reflections of the city lights. It was even more unusual for them to be alone. This was romantic as the dickens.

"I love you Becky. I can hardly believe what is happening to us." He was feeling joyous and humble at the same time as he held her hand.

"I know that you do my sweet man." Her eyes were sparkling. "You agreed to have a glass of wine with me. This must be a special evening. I love you too. You are guiding us in a dream come true. The days before we met seem so drab now. Did I tell you that I met with Phil's wife Gwen. She asked me about color choices and offered some great suggestions." She sort of squinted and said more softly, "Would you like a king size bed in the master bedroom?"

"Wow, that's a playful thought. But it brings up a bunch of questions we haven't talked about, like a wedding date; would you like to schedule some counselor or pastor sessions beforehand? Would you like a church wedding?" He took a deep breath before saying, "And I don't even know where to start the discussion of intimacy and privacy."

"Those are exactly the things I've wondered how I could bring up with you. Ward, you are amazing. Just when I think it can't get any better than this, you show me that it can. How crucial is the completion of the reno to your idea of a wedding day?

"Just when I start to say it isn't crucial at all, I think about our living situation. I would not imagine me living with you, Sophie and your mom with one bathroom. Nor could I imagine us living with Steve and Nora. So, I guess my answer is it's pretty important. But Phil believes they will be finished by the end of the month so, it's only going to have a positive influence. I like it that you and Gwen are making decisions. I want you to feel as much ownership in the project as you want."

She smiled warmly and told him, "I have a pretty healthy savings account that I planned to use for a place for just Sophie and me. If she can find some good deals on furniture, may I invest in them?"

"Gracious yes, Sweetheart. I have always thought that marriage partners should tell or discuss, but not need to ask permission. It is our project, coequal." There was a quiet pause then he asked, "Tell me how you feel about setting a date. Everything else will hinge on that."

She smiled even more. "School is out June 12th. I think a Sunday afternoon June 14th wedding would be sensational. My preference would be to have Pastor Shannon officiate on the sky patio. I'd like us to be the first to do that. I think you told me there would be a maximum capacity up there for thirty people. If it is rainy, we can be downstairs." She giggled, "How's that for wrapping up some major decisions and we still have a half of a glass of wine left." Dusk had chased most of the boats off of the lake but the city lights were reflecting more beautifully than ever.

Ward smiled as he considered her answer. "You know, if we invite the Thursday evening group, and I can't imagine them not being invited, that's about half full. Your mom, Sophie, Steve. Nora, Nick and Pastor Shannon leave only about ten more. I can live with that, but maybe we could invite folks to a reception later in the downstairs. Then we could invite all our friends, students and colleagues.

"I love that idea!" Becky leaned over to kiss Ward. "That is really the best of both, isn't it?"

He nodded and said, "Maybe it would be a good opportunity for our Republican friends to see the completed project. That could kick-start the zip code invitations." He hoped he wasn't getting too complicated with the wedding reception idea.

"Would it be O.K. if we include the Gig Harbor Rhodes?" She wasn't sure how appropriate that might be.

"There's that permission thing," Ward said warmly. "Do they love you and Sophie?"

"Yes, of course they do, but..."

Before she could finish her sentence, Ward chuckled, "Then they should be invited to the wedding. They are family. They want the best for you girls, and we can show them how comfortable the best can be."

Once again she came over to kiss him. "Thank you for loving me, and showing me how pleasant dreams can be. I'm just a little worried that something is going to interfere."

Confidently Ward said, "Fear is the thief of dreams. We are a dream team. There is nothing that can stop us." Then shyly he asked, "Wait, when was your period?"

She ruffled his hair, chuckling, "I've been on the pill for years. It helps with lighter and shorter periods." Then allowing her warm smile to blossom, she added, "But that does brig up another subject. What do you think about children? Would you like a larger family?"

"That's a simple answer. Yes, of course a family would be wonderful." Ward's gaze was direct. "The when of it might require some conversation." This dinner for two had taken longer and covered much more scope than they had expected, but warmly welcomed.

Saturday evening was date night at Lois'. She prepared a crab soufflé that was outstanding. Ward even enjoyed a glass of white wine with it. The greater joy, however, was the open discussion about the wedding. Several times Ward had to remind folks that they preferred a simple calm wedding and not a social sensation.

Monday morning the second period Algebra class found a Tootsie Roll on every desk again. The question was asked if they had done their exercises. All hands were raised. "Do your answers agree with these on the board? Raise your hands." Again all hands were raised with considerable humor. "Enjoy your prize. I'm proud to be in a class of awesome students," Ward said. The students understood that there was less humor and more praise in those words. "Let's use the rest of our hour on other less interesting subjects." Now that was funny!

A New Path

Ward arrived at the district offices five minutes early. He still had no clue what the meeting might entail, but he was fairly convinced that he had nothing to hide or regret. He was directed to an inner office and told it would only be a couple minutes until Dr. Anthony finished a call. On the wall Ward found pictures of a USC basketball team with Brad Anthony listed as an All American forward. They had finished third in the Final Four in '94. There were several other pictures that led Ward to understand that Dr. Anthony had been an outstanding collegiate athlete.

When his door opened he didn't quite duck, but at 6' 7" Dr. Anthony was impressive. His stature sort of made Ward feel like a cub scout. "Mr. Winter, I'm glad we finally get to meet. I've heard from several of your friends and if you are half as wonderful as they tell me, we are going to have a great time together." As they shook hands, Ward was aware of the largeness of Dr. Anthony's hand, and the care with which he had grasped the smaller hand. Ward liked this giant immediately. "Come in and be comfortable. I am eager to get to know you."

For a few minutes they talked about Ward's educational past, focusing on the assault and recovery. "Do I understand you have been at Roosevelt one year?"

Ward smiled and shrugged. "Well there was the year on probation prior to that. I basically took some refresher math classes and did substitute work."

"How is your recovery coming along?" The question was so sincere, Ward felt they were two old friends chatting."

"Just fine," he answered with a smile. "In Hawaii last month I strained the muscles in my hip. But that is pretty much healed."

"Do I understand you received that injury rescuing Dr. Rhodes' daughter?" The surprising question was asked with respect and admiration.

"Yes sir," Ward nodded. "She had strayed into some rougher water and a wave smacked her board into her face. I was grateful that her tether kept her from sinking deeper."

The administrator nodded and said, "Some folks are stymied by crisis. I heard that you knew exactly what to do and saved the little girl's life." His gaze at Ward was pure admiration.

"It was just the two of us there at that moment. She needed me and thankfully I was able to comply." He was feeling a bit uneasy about the topic but waited for another question.

The superintendent surprised Ward by saying, "Well pal, I haven't talked to one person, with the exception of Jim Reese, who doubts that you can walk on water, or meet any challenge. Tell me what are your plans for the summer?" Now the look in Dr. Anthony's eyes were direct and serious.

Ward, on the other hand chuckled. "I think this is going to be my summer to remember." He practically snorted. "We are just finishing a two hundred thousand dollar renovation to an old Green Lake home, June fourteenth Dr. Rhodes and I will be married, and wonderfully I will get to adopt that darling girl I rescued as my daughter." He took a deep breath and added, "Oh yes, I will assist the Seattle Republicans in a series of neighborhood promotions, and King County has allowed me to become a Marriage Clerk so I can officiate weddings on our sky patio." That made Dr. Anthony laugh out loud.

"Well brother, what are you going to do in your spare time?" the superintendent asked brightly. It was like he was speaking to an old friend.

Ward relaxed a bit seeing the direction of the conversation. He answered, "The word that comes to mind is 'adapt'. I'm not used to sharing the bathroom with anyone, let alone a nine year old princess." He hoped that wasn't too much information.

"Let's get down to the reason you are here today," Dr. Anthony said with a warm smile. "Because of your fortitude and integrity, Mr. Reese is no longer employed by our school district. His quick exit was in an agreement for us to forego charges of fraud against him. His resume was completely phony. In fact, the man only had an Associate degree from a Sacramento Community College. He pulled the wool over our eyes big time, much to the embarrassment of our HR process. The encounter with you, and your willingness to stand up to him, simply lifted the veil of deception. As HR did a better job with their back-checking, they uncovered the hoax. There is more than one change happening in our district system.

"Dr. Dave Tom has requested this meeting because he has nominated you to become the new Vice Principal for Roosevelt." Ward caught his breath. "We have examined your academic record and see that your Master's is solid and meets the requirement for the job. There are however three or four required subjects that you would need to complete, mainly in Administration and Human Resources. They could be done wholly or in part on-line. Dr. Jameson, who is one of the many supporters of the suggestion, has said with just a bit more effort, you could qualify for a doctorate. So, here's the plan we have come up with: For the next two school-years, you will continue to teach mornings and spend the afternoons as the Vice Principal. That would give you ample time to complete the requirements. Mr. Tom will be happy to help you with duties, schedules and expectations. I believe that could be an ideal transition. Upon this first hearing, what are your thoughts?"

Ward took in a deep breath and smiled. "It sounds a little risky," he replied. "But I think the greatest hazard in life is to risk nothing, which accomplishes nothing." He looked at Dr. Anthony's serious face and said, "Becky and I will pray about this tonight. I'm sure she will agree that it is a great challenge and opportunity. I will be honored to accept this plan." He nodded his head to punctuate the answer.

"Terrific!" the administrator declared with enthusiasm. He reached out his hand to shake Ward's again. "Now that we have the tough stuff out of the way, may I ask you a theoretical question?"

"Of course," Ward was glad the big stuff had been accomplished so easily.

"Olympia is wrestling with the issue of gay marriage. If it should become law, would you be willing to conduct a wedding ceremony on the sky patio, I think you called it, for my partner and me?"

In just that instant Ward saw Dr. Anthony not as a college athlete, conference all star hero, but a man with a burden just like all the rest of us. "Of course I would," he said boldly. "But I must warn you that the patio maximum capacity is only thirty people. For larger groups we would need to use the commons room downstairs. That can hold about a hundred and fifty folks." His smile never faded and Dr. Anthony understood that it was a genuine answer.

"I admire you, Ward. I can see the quality that has made you an outstanding teacher and friend to your students. Let's agree to meet again next Tuesday the nineteenth at the same time and there will be a few more folks to set this assignment in motion. O.K.?"

As they stood up, Ward said respectfully, "You have got to be the tallest man I've ever met."

"Yeah, I had three good years, then I blew out my knee and ended my career. I still hold some high point records at SC." He paused and Ward thought their conversation was finished. Then Dr. Anthony said softly, with a catch in his voice, "But I never saved a little girl from drowning. Which achievement do you think is greater?" Before he could answer Dr. Anthony patted his shoulder and directed him to the door. Ward had so much to talk about with Becky.

But before that could happen, Nora told him as soon as he got home that a Mrs. Jameson had requested he return her call.

"Hello Mrs. Jameson, It's Ward Winter returning your call. Mom suggested you have a question for me." He was once again wondering where this might take him.

"Ward it is Peggy; we are much better friends than that formality. I must confess that I have been so caught up in the Roosevelt stuff that I failed to remind you about our second quarter caucus meeting. I'm afraid that I might be too late to get you and Becky to join us again. It is just next Sunday at the Sheraton. Please tell me there is a chance that you can be our guests again. Bob has told me about your agreement to take responsibility for the neighborhood meetings. That is so wonderful. I would love to hear about it at our table. Will you consider it please?" Her voice was warm and a bit desperate.

"Peggy, I can't speak for Becky, but I'm sure I can be there. Do I remember that the program begins at 7 o'clock?" He was pretty sure Becky would want to be there too, but it was best that she determined that for herself.

"You are an angel!" she breathed a sigh of relief. "And Ginger tells me your tough side is pretty wonderful too. I heard that Reese is gone after a run-in with you."

"No ma'am," he said quickly. "I don't think I had much to do with Mr. Reese's self -implosion, except lie my face off in defense of those innocent guys. I've heard that it was a dad that painted the window; he was furious at Mr. Reese. There really was no malicious damage to the school, only to the Principal's ego."

"I know why Ginger adores you," the happy mom added. "You remind me of the good old days when character and charm could live together. I'll be ever so glad to see you again."

Ward was left wondering about her meaning or if she was just trying to be cordial.

Later, when he called Becky to check on her availability, she answered, "Oh my goodness! I can dimly recall the days before you came into my life when nothing was happening to my calendar. Now it seems I'm like a climber in the Himalayas. There are more mountaintops than I can recall and each one seems more dramatic or important than the previous one." She paused for just a moment, then said, "Of course I want to be with you Sunday evening. I have no idea what I could have to share, but just being with you is satisfying these days. Do you mind being my hero?"

He repeated her words, "I also have no idea what I have to share, but being with you is always inspiring to me." He paused, wishing he could give her a kiss. "Good, I'll call Peggy to confirm us."

Spring days are chronologically longer, but the busy agenda makes them fly by quicker. Phil had daily questions about final finish colors and incidentals. Gwen called Becky two or three times every day, usually with an amazing find that would be a treasure. She also had many suggestions from Overstock liquidation for pots and pans, dishes and glassware. It was obvious the completion day was at hand.

Once again the Sheraton welcomed them with its splendor, "It's amazing," Ward whispered as though he would disturb those around him. I see so much that I missed last time. This is just plain spectacular."

Becky giggled, which is it, plain or spectacular?"

"You know what I mean. I can't look at it all at once." They made their way to the third floor and found Peggy standing by their assigned table. She happily waved them over.

"It is so good to see you both again," she said nearly singing it. "You know where Bob is. He really loves being part of this, but isn't very comfortable if there is disagreement. I think our table drew the short straw; our table discussion is 'Homelessness.' There is bound to be a variety of opinions." She looked at Ward saying, "I'm counting on you to have some solid idea instead of the cookie cutter stuff we have come up with in the past." She gave them both a sincere hug.

Ward recognized Mr. Jensen. The banker came directly over to greet them and announce that Home and Garden had paid their third and half of the remaining fees. "I can't recall a plan that has been as trouble free as this one. You must have a lucky star." He shook Ward's hand and returned to his table.

As he walked away Ward whispered to Becky, "I do have a lucky star. I last saw it over Hawaii." They shared a chuckle.

The lights dimmed, Bob hurried to the table and the opening greeting was just like the last time, and equally stirring. A serving person came by to take their drink orders and Becky requested two diet cokes, just like the last time.

The first presenter was a woman who spoke about the cyclical pattern of American politics. For the last decade Republicans had increased the military budget and lowered the debt even during a time of unrelenting warfare. Now the Democrats have a minority candidate running against a war hero, John McCain. By the rhetoric we can expect expanded government and increase to the national debt.

The second presenter talked about the danger of government regulations to the detriment of private enterprise. Ward liked that fellow a lot and wished he could speak longer.

The final presenter used a variety of tender stories to whip up enthusiasm for partisan cooperation between the two parties. A dangerous trend toward obstruction and ideology differences was lessening the effectiveness of congress. Neither party seemed willing to compromise. The prognosis was that many necessary bills, including the budget, were stalled in committees and might require emergency attention.

It was time for a break before the round-table discussion. Bob announced that the topic was homelessness, which didn't seem to produce a lot of eagerness. "This time, let's go left around the table." Ward wondered if he had talked too long last time.

Becky began by saying, "I think the homeless camps have brought a degree of community to the issue. I heard that the one in the parking lot of St. Rose is doing real well. The congregation has sponsored dinners and opens its bathroom facilities for them." She glanced at Ward suggesting she was finished.

He grinned and said, "We are to be married in just a month, so at the risk to marital bliss, I need to see the problem as two different issues." She gave him a good natured elbow. "First I see the problem as protection of sanitation and property rights. Secondly as a condition of addiction. Choice is another name for fate and destiny is its consequences. The rampant evidence of drug use by discarded needles and human waste is an unavoidable sign. Alcoholism by cans and bottles carelessly scattered speaks of another facet of the same huge problem. There are the unemployed and then there are the unemployable due to the consequences of their addiction. Garbage and feces creates an immediate health problem. I think Vagrancy should be seen as a crime, surely it is a wasted life. Shifting the sites for larger and more camps only proliferates the problem by attracting more vagrants and uses more valued property and budget funds. Seattle is running out of space for the healthy stuff that wants to grow here. I think if vagrants could be arrested, which removes their choice in the matter, and transferred to a low security recovery facility they could be separated from their source of alcohol or drugs and get clean for once. That could change their destiny to one of productivity. I can imagine a felony charge that would require six months in detox, then another six months in job training and personal care. Shifting them from one place after another only costs the city millions each year in cleanup and is like shoveling sand against the tide. I think it is an individual problem that depends on a great deal of social support."

The man sitting next to Ward nodded and said, "I agreed with Miss Rhodes. But I think this guy has a solution based concept. The camps only let them continue. The other day I drove along Harbor Avenue over by Salty's. In a two block range, I counted over a dozen RV's up on leveling jacks obviously parked there for a while taking up needed spaces.

We never used to see stuff like that. Without septic hookups they were dropping their waste on the street. That's disgusting. I do think that should be against the law."

The woman next to him said, "Yes it should, but the camps are at least an effort to do something organized. It's better to light a candle, as they say. Without the camps they were under bridges and using abandoned buildings."

The woman next to her said, "Yes, and with the camps they still are. I don't understand how squatters can just take over a place, like the old Tribune Building. How can they say that it is their right to just move into a space. There have been a number of fires there and the building is scheduled to be destroyed, but they are still there. Pictures show a deplorable mess of trash and waste inside the old building. I think I like his idea of making it against the law."

The man next to her shook his head saying, "It's those damned panhandlers that get me. We have a couple guys who set up their tent right on the sidewalk in front of our building. Usually one of them is sitting out there, begging for money when I get off of work. The news told a story about a lady who stands on the corner by the Fifth Ave theater, before and after shows. She's crying and holding a sign that says her children are hungry. Last year, according to the news, she took in over a hundred thousand dollars! Think of that! I'll bet she didn't pay a penny of tax on it. I think that's like robbery."

The next lady said quietly, "How could you dream of making poverty a crime? I always feel better when I have opened my hand to someone less fortunate." Her gaze was on Ward. "Then should we arrest the people who are under the poverty level for a misdemeanor?" She shook her head.

The man sitting next to Peggy said. "I've been thinking about what you said." He was looking at Ward. "When people receive the consequences of their bad decisions they rarely admit their mistake. They try to blame someone else or some condition beyond their control. There are already a lot of programs to help the homeless, but they refuse them saying that it's their free choice. I like the notion that denial is shot to hell if we make it a felony. That's serious. Two more and it's for life. Yeah, I see how that could be a real workable thing, even a new model for recovery."

Peggy said, "I don't know, Ward. I think there are many addictions like lying, gambling, sex that are life altering but we would never make them a felony. But I guess what you are implying is that the homeless are a unique problem because they invade other's property. I do like your idea of detox though. That might help the patient deal more responsibly with his problem."

Dr, Jameson concluded the circle by saying, "There is an Edmond Burke quote I have used often. "The only thing necessary for the triumph of evil is for the good person to do nothing." He looked at each person seated at the table. "This has been a fascinating conversation. I appreciate each of your viewpoints. Peggy will pass these along so that they can get a clear picture of how complex the issue is. Remember the summer caucus will be September 7th, just after school starts."

The man sitting beside Peggy obviously wasn't ready to leave the discussion, for he asked Ward, "You have me thinking. If a detox center wouldn't be built here, where would you think it might go?"

Ward shrugged, "There must be a bunch of places within an easy hundred mile radius from here where property values are much more affordable. For example, a bank has been trying to sell the whole town of Zillah over in the Yakima valley. That property would be affordable, accessible and in an agricultural area where labor jobs should be available. I think that would be great. It could also become a source of financial growth for that area with new jobs and homes."

Dr. Jameson thanked the table for their loyal attendance and participation. He added, "Ward, at the first caucus you gave us some food for thought. Tonight You brought us more to think about, and we are still leaving as friends."

Ward responded, "I once heard a speaker say that the truth will set us free, but first it will make us pretty angry. My strong belief is that information is neutral; it's what we do with it that sets the tone of our relationship. I'm just grateful that we are still friends here." His smile was gracious.

On the way home he asked Becky if he had again spoken too much. She assured him that she liked to think about what he had to share. "Most of us just had notions about the subjects. It was like we put our prejudices on parade. You had given it some serious thought and offered a solution. You may have spoken more than the rest of us, but that was because we didn't have more to say." She put her hand on his leg with a pat.

The late news reported a disturbance at Giggles. The information was still being gathered but apparently two gangs had been inside when a fight erupted. There were several serious injuries and considerable damage to the club. It would be closed for repairs until further notice.

Fourth period Trig class was filing out. Ward's smile was reflecting his anticipation of chatting with Becky about the progress of supplying furniture. She had told him that Gwen was negotiating for a remarkable cherry dining room set.

His attention was drawn to a student who hadn't folded her notebook and simply remained seated looking sad. "Ann, is everything O.K.?" he asked her. She simply stared at him and still didn't move. "I'm thinking there is something wrong. May I help you?" he asked now with more focus.

She dried her eyes with a Kleenex. "I don't think anyone can help." Now she put her face in her hands and shuddered.

Ward moved near her and asked softly, "Can you tell me what has you so shaken."

In a tiny voice the girl whispered, "I didn't do anything to deserve this and no one will believe me."

Ward placed his hand on her shoulder and said softly, "I will believe you and I can help. Did you know that on break, I saved a little girl from drowning? I still have hero status. Now come on, Ann. Share your problem with me and we can work it out." A long silence lingered before she met his eyes and attempted a tiny smile.

She looked at her hands and finally told him, "Norm and I went to a Christmas party together. It was nice. But since then what he has been sending me is not nice. It started playfully and then got nasty, ugly. He has been telling his friends terrible lies about me and threatening me if I won't do stuff with him. He has called me nasty names." She shook her head in desperation.

"May I see your phone?" Ward asked softly. "I won't open any texts, but I would like to see the history cache." She reached in her purse and produced the phone. It only took him a minute to see how many texts she had received. "Do you know what class Norm has now?" His tone was caring and gentle.

"I think he has PE this hour, with Mr. Shelton." Her face was still sad but her hope was moving the storm clouds of tears from her eyes.

"Let's not worry about this anymore, O.K.?" his smile was reassuring. "This is just between you and me. We don't need any more to fix it. But if you get one more ugly text from him, let me know. Then we will bring in the big guns. O.K.?" He gave her shoulder a little pat of encouragement.

Ward immediately went to Mr. Shelton's gym class, walked in and asked to see Norm Vladyka immediately. The young man was identified and Ward asked him to come out into the hallway for a minute.

"Norm I don't want you to say a word. Is that understood?" Ward said in an ominous quiet voice. When the puzzled student nodded, Ward continued. "I have just had a painful conversation with Ann Meeker, who tells me you like to send dirty lies about her, that you are a potty-mouth with absolutely no respect or conscience." His voice was calm and controlled, which had a chilling effect on his listener, who began shaking his head. "She wants to never hear from you again, in any way. Is that clear to you?" The lad nodded. "I'm not sure you understand how much trouble you are in, so let me make it real clear. If she receives one more text or email from you of any sort, if you tell one more of your creepy little friends an untruth about her, I will personally make sure you are charged with being a bully and a sexual predator. Any future that you might hope to have will be impossible. You and your family will be disgraced. Is that clear to you?" Tears were running down the young man's face. "Do not try to apologize to her in any way or try to talk your sleazy way out of this. You are busted. If you don't believe me, next time you will be talking to a judge." Ward turned and walked away leaving a young man in shock and remorse.

By the time school let out for the afternoon, most of the senior class girls had heard the word that Mr. Winter doesn't mince around with bullies. "He has your back and is not slow to prove it."

It was impossible for Ward to stay away from Winter Place; it was so near completion. Now that the new parking area had been installed it was like a different place. Shoot! It was a completely different place. He was challenged to completely believe that it would be their house, for their family. It made him grin to let that reality sink in. Phil had said that the renovation would be all wrapped up in just nine more days. Then the TV crew would have two days to complete their filming. It was scheduled to air in the fall as their new season opener.

After supper Ward called Becky to share with her his accomplishments of the day. With a sigh he began, "Today I only thought about you seventy seven thousand times" They both chuckled. "I did get the three Admin books for my on-line requirement. So far I have only had time to glance at them, but it looks really doable. The exciting thing is that I made our reservations for Kenmore Air to fly us to Victoria Sunday evening the 14th. They will deliver us right to the Custom's dock. We can either walk the three blocks or take a water taxi over to the Ocean Point Resort."

Becky asked, "Is the water taxi quicker as well as easier? I think I would like the most direct transportation." She giggled, "It sounds like another dream."

Ward continued, "We'll fly back on Tuesday afternoon. Have you asked Sophie what she would like for her three days?" He had suggested either a short trip to the Oregon coast or a stay at Sky Ranch in Ellensburg. There she could learn to ride a horse and play with the goats.

"I'm not sure she is completely over the Hawaii trip," Becky said softly. "I thought it was gracious of you to suggest that the three of us have a couple days together," she said. "But Sophie's answer was, 'What's wrong with staying in our new big house?' She finally agreed that if you want to, you can take us to the zoo or the aquarium."

When there was a quiet pause, Ward said, "Twenty seven days, can you believe it? Some of the time I believe it couldn't possibly be true. I guess this is what is meant by 'my cup runeth over.'" They continued to chat for almost an hour.

The second meeting with Dr. Anthony caught Ward by surprise. Oh, not the time or date of course, but by the number of important folks who were in attendance. When he arrived at the District office he was invited to go right in, the meeting was already in progress.

"Come in Ward," Mr. Anthony said with a happy smile. I believe you know Dr. Tom, the new Roosevelt Principal and Dr. Charlie Stanton, our comptroller. Let me introduce Dr. Kim Lee, the Director of Human Resources and Jan Conner my Administrative Assistant, with whom you have chatted a couple times. Do you feel you are before a firing Squad?" His smile was a great start even though Ward had no idea how this was going to conclude.

The Superintendant was in charge of the agenda so he informed Ward, "Your teaching accomplishments are before us, but obviously they are limited to this year. One striking thing that we all noted was that by the start of the second semester, the two other algebra classes were also functioning at a near perfect rate. We have never seen this level of proficiency. Can we assume that you have something to do with that change?"

Ward smiled confidently, "You may recall that I said the idea of Tootsie Rolls came from a faculty meeting. It started as something of a joke, but the results were hard to overlook. As teachers, we are friends, not in competition with one another. So when they suggested they might try it, I encouraged them. It is both playful, and an undeniable reward for extra effort on the student's part. If you ask me if it is right or a sound teaching principle, I'd only be able to point to the results. If the end justifies the means, I believe it has changed me dramatically as a teacher." He felt that was answer enough.

"Tell me this," Dr. Anthony continued. "Do you think it would work on all disciplines, history English, biology for example?"

Ward shrugged. "Dr. Anthony, I'm not theorist enough to even guess. I just know that we needed some boost in math enthusiasm, and Tootsie Rolls did the job."

"You know what's funny?" the Administrator asked. Ward broke into a big grin because he knew the answer was 'No'. Mr. Anthony reported, "I have been contacted by the marketing manager of Tootsie Rolls for an interview. It seems we are a new practical application for their product." He chuckled, "We have a rare situation here. Mr. Tom has assured me that your action taken recently with Mr. Reese was completely in the best interest of the Roosevelt students, including providing a phony alibi for two of the accused boys. Everyone in this room believes that your mercy was a higher justice. That's why we all have approved of the unusual promotion we have offered you."

In the following minutes each one explained their expectations for Ward's involvement as combination teacher and Assistant Principal. They offered steps to make it a permanent promotion. Finally, Dr. Anthony complimented everyone for their participation and said, "We have only one more task to complete. Ward we need you to sign your new contract. Your new salary will begin with the new school year."

Dr. Lee offered him a folder with the documents. One page at a time, she carefully explained their function. "Now with your signature, we are all done here."

Ward looked at each of them sitting around the table. Finally he said, "But I can't sign this." He frowned and the others were puzzled. "This contract says that I have ten years of seniority, which would put me in a higher compensation level. That's not right. I have only one and one of probation." He shrugged. It wasn't his fault.

"Well darn it all," Dr. Anthony growled. "That means you need to come back next week to complete the contract. Will that be an inconvenience?"

"Even if it were," Ward said lightly, "Like the commercial says, 'You only have one chance to make a first impression.' I want my impression to be spot on correct."

"Well said," the tall Superintendant praised. He thanked everyone for setting aside this time. He was well satisfied, even if they would need yet another appointment to complete the task.

As soon as Ward got home he called Becky to share the outcome of the meeting.

She asked him for clarity, "You say there was an error in your contract? That is really strange. Dr. Lee is my supervisor, and is known for her thoroughness. But it was good that you all discovered it before signing. They are really difficult to modify once completed." They talked for several more minutes. Before Becky told Ward how much their love meant to her and how much he was on her mind, she mentioned that the ladies from table fifteen were coming over Thursday evening for pizza. She wanted them to be personally invited to the wedding.

After supper Ward called the other fellows from table fifteen to invite them to a Thursday night pizza dinner at his place. He wanted to invite them personally to the wedding, and ask Jay to be his best man.

Wednesday afternoon Ward stayed in the faculty room after the other teachers had left. He had found that it was a perfect out-of-the-way place to study his administration books. The school was nearly deserted except for the custodians. He was startled when a pretty face peeked in and asked, "Mr. Winter, will you help me please?"

He thought her name was Christina, because it reminded him of his sister, but she was not in his algebra class. "How can I help you?"

"I've missed my bus, and my folks are out of town. Do you think you could give me a ride home?" Her sweet smile seemed innocent.

"Where do you live, Chrissy?" It seemed like only a small problem. It was about to get considerably larger.

She entered the room and moved close to Ward. "Mmmm, my dad calls me that," she said softly. "It warms my heart." Her smile became even warmer. "Just up in Bridle Trails, but it's too far to walk."

"How did you manage to miss your bus?" he asked.

"Larry and I were in the library and I sort of lost track of time. When I'm with a nice guy that can happen. I'd really appreciate a ride. You could come in for a while if you'd like." Her innocent gaze was setting off alarm bells in Ward.

"Let's call a taxi for you. I'll pay the fare." He thought that might be an excessive solution, but a safe one.

She stepped a bit too close to Ward and whispered, "If you are willing to pay, I can be awfully nice to you too. Please take me home."

A wave of fear and nausea hit Ward. This was almost as bad as Theresa Tran. "Christina, to be clear are you offering me a sexual experience with you?" His voice was trembling, but not in a good way.

"Please Mr. Winter, I need the money. I'll do anything you like for twenty five dollars." A tear traced down her cheek but she held her gaze.

Ward took a couple deep breathes, thinking, then he said "Christina, this is wrong in so many ways. You are not that sort of person. I can tell that you are smart and kind and not in any way crass enough to be anything other than a sweet Roosevelt student. What is going on here? Because you have solicited me, I now must report you to the police. But I don't think that is going to end it, will it?" His expression became less serious. With only another moment's thought he picked up the phone and called the Wallingford police.

Her face paled, "Oh please don't do that Mr. Winter. Please don't..."

"Good afternoon Officer Nunez. I'm Ward Winter, teacher here at Roosevelt. I have an awkward situation. One of my students just solicited me for a sexual experience, asking me for a specific amount. I must report that, which I am doing now." He listened and answered, "Her name is Krista Clark, I believe," he lied. "But I'm not sure." He listened again. "Yes, here in the faculty room." After a brief moment he answered, "No there has been no physical contact of any sort." He listened again and wrote down a complaint number. "Officer Nunez, may I request a service from you. Will you please call the Superintendant of Seattle Schools?" Ward gave him the number. "Please ask Dr. Bradley Anthony if this is part of a personnel investigation. In any case, he should be informed of the complaint immediately." Ward listened again and smiled. "I understand, sir, and totally agree. Your job is much too demanding than to chase shadows and false complaints. I'm sure Dr. Anthony will want to hear that assessment." He hung up the phone and looked at a young lady who was staring at the floor.

"How did you know?" she asked softly.

"Sweetie," Ward acted shocked, "you are forgetting that I am a super hero teacher. I can see into your soul and all I find there is pure niceness, not a shred of that ugly tawdry stuff. I believe in you, even though that was an award winning act for a couple minutes."

Now she looked at him with a smile. "But wasn't I even a little believable? I'm in the drama class and thought it was pretty good."

"You were far too good," Ward explained, "scary good. But there have been a couple other scenes that have happened to me in the last week that caused me to look deeper into it."

She asked if she could give him an apologetic hug. "I'm sorry for the implications. I was pretty sure you would find a way around my invitation."

"To be able to swear in court, if it should ever come to that, that I never touched you, I must decline. But," Ward's grin grew, "I'll tell you what I will give you for your winning performance, however." He reached into his briefcase and handed her a Tootsie Roll.

She was laughing as she left the room.

During their evening phone conversation, Ward told Becky about the incident. At first she was alarmed. There were few acceptable categories for such a personal episode. "Was she explicit in her offer?" Becky asked more alarmed than curious, but a bit of both.

Ward said, "Not graphic, but she did say she would do anything for twenty five dollars." He softened his voice and said honestly, "That was explicit enough to embarrass me."

She was quiet for a moment then said as though she were asking herself, "I wonder if you are correct and all those things have been generated by Dr. Anthony. It seems pretty extreme, don't you think?" Her voice seemed small and troubled.

Ward answered, "I'm sure it's outside anything I expected. I'll even bet that the error on my contract is part of his plot. But when I talk to you I know that worry doesn't erase the pain of tomorrow, it drains the joy from today. So, no worries! I have an appointment with Superintendant Anthony next Tuesday. I'll bet the rest of the picture will be clear then. Let's talk about something more fun, like the completion of the reno. By the end of next week it will be all done. Phil says he has a very short punch-list."

Becky's voice brightened. "And Gwen says she has at least two truckloads of furniture for us. It feels like Christmas because so much of it will be something of a surprise. She found two sets of teak office furniture for the downstairs offices, desks, bookcases and credenzas. She says we will be blown away by it."

"Can you recall how bleak and empty the house was not long ago?" Ward asked softly. "Accepting this much change will be overwhelming by itself." They chatted for several more minutes, never mentioning again the episode of the afternoon. But silently, Becky gave thanks that this man she loved could be so open to talk with her about it.

Saturday evening was another "date night." Nick had claimed the privilege of hosting a dinner at Salty's on Harbor Way. They were glad for a late spring sunset because the skyline of Seattle was reflecting back to them. Their conversation, however, was brighter. Ward shared that the renovation would be complete by Wednesday and Gwen would move in all her purchases by Friday. He wanted to giggle or weep, but was satisfied with a broad smile. "May I invite you all to the inaugural pizza dinner at Winter Place?"

Monday afternoon Steve, Nora, Lois, Becky, Florence, and Jay each received a call from Dr. Anthony. He asked them directly if Ward had said anything at all to them about a bullying situation at school, a mistake on his contract, or an inappropriate solicitation from a student, or, he asked only at the last, anything about the Superintendent's sexual orientation. All but Becky assured him that Ward had mentioned not a word about any of those situations. Becky told him honestly that they had discussed the mistake on his contract and the solicitation and quick resolution. He assured them all that Ward was an above average man of honor and respectability and thanked them for their time.

When Ward walked into her office at 2:15, Mrs. Conner met him with a warm smile and said "Punctual as usual. He is expecting you Mr. Winter." That made Ward smile too.

"Come in Ward, come on in," he was greeted. As he entered the office Ward realized that Dr. Lee was there again. "Please be comfortable. You remember Dr. Lee from HR," the superintendent said. He then began an apology that cleared up several questions from the previous days. "Now will you forgive me?" he asked honestly. "I can't remember ever pulling a stunt like that. But let me begin by saying that my motives were honorable. With most advancements like you are receiving, we have several years of service to identify personal strengths and weaknesses. We haven't that privilege with you, so I improvised. Brother, you are cool. My gosh! What did it take you fifteen minutes to quiet a troubled woman who was being bullied and set the table square with her adversary. That was textbook. Ann said she knew you were listening to her and sympathetic to her fears. Christina tells me that you scarcely blinked when she tried to seduce you. I am impressed, Ward. By the way, those three students are from your drama department and gave themselves top marks for believability. Norm said he was actually frightened by your intensity."

Dr. Lee took over by saying, "On average less than half of the candidates we see read their contract. One out of ten who find a mistake in their favor call our attention to it. I think that puts you in the top five percent of folks who have critical integrity. It took you only the time I explained the documents for you to catch the error of a ten instead of a one. I also am impressed and encouraged that there are still people of honor.

"The other test that most of the folks I know would have failed, you aced," Dr. Anthony said with a soft voice. "When I gave you the misinformation that I am gay, that could have spread far and wide in minutes. I called a half dozen of your family and friends and learned that not one of them, even Dr. Rhodes who is about to become your bride, was made privy to that information. I am more than impressed. I am dumbfounded. You shared that information with not a single soul. Integrity, courage, honesty and diversity are each qualities that we covet. You have demonstrated all four. I'm not sure I know anyone else who could have passed those tests." Dr. Lee was nodding in agreement.

"The frosting on the cake for me, Ward," Dr. Anthony continued with a chuckle, "is the fact that you had class enough to send Officer Nunez to scold me for causing an official complaint to become a personnel device. To say that our conversation was friendly would be an overstatement, you scoundrel. I believe you knew how that was going to snap back on me. Good job!"

He looked at Dr. Lee and said," I believe Ward is the ideal candidate for Roosevelt. Do you agree?" She nodded and opened her folder, producing a corrected contract. When Ward signed it his salary and responsibilities increased substantially. He had two years to complete his academic requirements. They shook hands.

As Ward was walking toward the door, Dr. Anthony said, "Ward, my marital status is actually promising right now. I would love a tour of your new home, especially the sky patio. Kathleen and I have been talking about venues for a wedding. Without a church choice we have been thinking about a banquet site. Would you be open to the possibility…?" he left the question unfinished.

"I would be honored, sir," Ward answered. "I'm on my way over there right now. I believe the renovation is just hours from completion. Becky and I have made a tentative schedule of events for the house. June sixth is on our calendar as an informal open house for family and friends. The contractor has told me that there has already been a half dozen realtors offering to list it for sale. I believe you will be impressed by it. I'll send you the details." Once again they shook hands. Ward had the strange feeling that they were good friends. Brad would have agreed with that feeling.

When he arrived at Winter Place, Ward was delighted to see a moving truck in the lower parking unloading folding tables and three large caddies of folding chairs. Apparently Mrs. Murphy wanted to be ready to invite the Republicans as soon as possible. On the Winona Ave side of the house another team of men were unloading another van of furniture. Gwen was equally eager.

Phil's big smile was a happy sign to Ward. The contractor greeted him with a firm handshake, saying, "I'm really glad to see you. This job is done! Well, except for the cleaning crew that will be here in the morning before the film crew. They have almost all the finished footage they need so I will ask you to give them one more day before you bring folks through." He chuckled, "You might need a big stick to beat off the realtors. There are a couple really pushy ones who insist they have buyers waiting to meet you."

"Let's go upstairs for a walk through. By the way, do you like the flagpole at the corner of the house," he pointed. "We still have twenty thousand unspent dollars. I thought it was a nice touch. I'll remove it if you would choose not to have it."

Ward was thinking about the many Republicans who would welcome that patriotic symbol and he was one of them for sure. "That's a super addition," he replied.

On the sky patio, Phil advised a gray wood treatment every two years. "If you will do that these 2 X 6 planks will last a very long time." Then he pointed to another surprise. "This area will be a very sunny spot so we added an Arbor with a retractable sun shade. If you are going to have weddings up here," his smile widened, "I think some hanging flower pots would be all the trimming you might need." He demonstrated how the awning cranked out and retracted.

They went through the French doors to the master bedroom. Ward grinned when he saw the king size bed and dresser. "Let me show you the show stopper shower," Phil continued their tour. "I think this might be my favorite highlight and there are a lot of them." They worked their way through the entire home until they were back in the commons. "The big screen plasma TV is all wired into the cable. You'll just need to order service to it. There is a double lock security closet around the corner here, with power and a DVD player. There is also a pretty nice PA system. She set you up for success."

As Phil stepped out the double doors back into the parking are he said, "There are a couple more surprises I'd like to show you." He pushed the doorbell switch and from a back room came a loud bark of a dog. "You can change the response to a chime similar t the upstairs if you like. I thought this might be unique enough to be a novelty." He pressed it again and Ward had to grin because he really liked the sound of a big nasty dog, like Franny. Phil concluded the walk-through by pointing out, "The suspended entrance cover makes this look sort of commercial. But it's the most effective shelter we could add without posts or walls. Oh, there is one more thing. Your garage door openers also have a switch for the security fence. Just hit the rocker switch on the side and the gate will glide open or closed. Make sure you keep that track clutter free because the gate has a safety switch. If it triggers, you'll just need to reset it with the rocker switch on the other side. I'm assuming this will not be used regularly, but it is cool too." Ward was nearly speechless from the wonders of this house, and it was his!

It only required four trips in his packed car to move the boxes from Steve's garage. Ward reminded himself that there was an easy tendency to allow clutter to build up. He definitely didn't want that to happen to this beautiful new place. Three of the boxes were text books that he was sure he would never open again and he asked himself why was he keeping them?

By Saturday morning he had his stuff fairly put away and the frig filled. Comcast had established the phone and cable connection so his first call was to Becky. "Good morning Beauty. Welcome to June! This is going to be the best month ever! If you guys haven't had breakfast, would you like to come over to Winter Place for some French toast and a walk through?" He heard her relay the invitation and an excited little girl's positive response.

"Mom says it will just take a few minutes to change into something more appropriate." She snickered, "We're still in our 'jamas. We can be there by nine. O,K,?"

"I'll put the tea water on, and tell Sophie that we have POG." He was about to say goodbye when he added, "Hey, park off Greenlake Way and use the downstairs doorbell. I hope you like it." He went through the house turning on lights.

When Ward opened the commons door, Sophie was nearly screaming, "Did we get a dog?" Her mom started to scold her but Ward said, "I felt the same way when I heard that big voice bark. I'm sorry if I played a trick on you. It's only a make-believe dog. But doesn't he sound real? If ever some bad person was trying to come into our house we could just say, 'Sic'em!' and I'll bet they would run away." That was at least enough to help her smile in understanding. "I've been thinking we should name our make-believe dog 'Magic.' What do you think?"

Becky said, "He fooled me. I almost forgot that there is POG in the kitchen." That brightened everyone. Before the hour was out they were familiar with every marvelous part of the house.

Sophie asked, "Daddy Ward, which bedroom is mine?"

"You have your choice of either one across from ours, with your own bathroom." His warm smile was shared by Becky who enjoyed the idea of "ours".

The sun was breaking through the morning overcast so they could stand on the sky patio and watch the folks walking around Greenlake. Several of the walkers even waved to them.

When they were back downstairs enjoying another cup of tea, Ward asked, "Lois, I have a tender question. As usual, I'm not sure how to start. I am disrupting your household. For over a decade you have been a very special group. I don't want to take away what is precious to you. I've been thinking that the guest bedroom down here would be a comfortable place for you, if you would like to join us." He knew it was awkward, but he also felt it was kind.

Lois put her hand on Ward's arm with a smile. "You are the most thoughtful person I know. Well, the most thoughtful man anyway." She glanced at Becky, then added, "I might not be so lonely after the wedding. Isn't it wonderful how things work out? Nick and I have been talking." Becky's smile bloomed into a joyful one. "He has convinced me that we both will benefit from your wedding. I'm thinking about selling my old house. He has asked me if I would consider marrying him and move to West Seattle."

"Mom!" Becky nearly sobbed with joy, "When were you going to tell me?" She came around the table to embrace her warmly. "I've worried about what you will do without us."

Lois sort of shrugged, "Yes, I've wondered about that too. I don't need the money. Your dad's insurance and pension have been taking care of us. I really like Nick and I was sorry to hear him say that he is very lonely. I don't even remember which one of us mentioned it first. Two lonely people in love is a good solution. You know, he even likes to dance but hasn't had a partner for years. I told him, 'Me too.' I think that's how it started." Her pursed lips gave a little grin.

As they were talking the chimes for the front door rang. When Ward opened the door, a smiling man offered him a business card saying, "Good morning. I'm Pete Graham from Windermere Realty. I see that the renovation is complete and I wonder if you have a selling agent. I have two different buyers who are very motivated to acquire this place." He was trying to look over Ward's shoulder to see the interior. "May I take a look at the completed project?"

Ward's smile didn't fade, but he didn't move either. "No, Pete, you may not. This house is not for sale. If you would like to see the interior, may I suggest you watch the fall premier of the Home and Garden Reno Masters series. They did a splendid coverage of it. Have a pleasant day." As he closed the door he was certain the realtor was trying to offer more reasons for the door to remain open.

Quickly returning to the kitchen table, Ward asked, "Lois, is there anything I can do to help you with Nick?"

His mom-in-law-to-be chuckled, "My, look at all you have already done. Since New Year's Eve we have been together almost every Saturday evening. We have worshipped together and prayed. We have talked on the phone nearly as much as you two and had a couple lunches you didn't know about. You have been the, what do they call it, catalyst for something very nice. And we are nearly as thrilled as you two are about the summer. We are just taking it slowly. He wants to be in touch with his son and daughter before we make any announcement." Her comfortable smile was warming to the others at the table.

The doorbell rang again. It was another realtor asking if he could show the house.

After Ward had again politely told the man this marvelous home was not for sale, he said to Becky, "If we are going to try to have some sort of open house next Saturday, I'd better get some invitation cards. There's not much time to get them in the mail."

She smiled and counter-offered, "If we make a list, I can email them a lot quicker. Since they almost all are from work or school, I've got their email addresses."

"I don't have many other suggestions," he said, "than Dr. Jameson and Peggy, Craig Jensen from the Washington Mutual and Mrs. Murphy. But if we get most of those folks, it will be a very fun open house."

Lois asked if she could help with food.

Ward answered, "I was thinking it would be easiest if I get two or three of those trays of turkey pinwheel sandwiches and some cookies from the store. If you could make sure the coffee pot is tended and a pitcher of punch, we might need two or three bottles of wine. Just tell me what you think we'll need for supplies and I'll take care of it." He was feeling a good enthusiasm for the idea.

Becky said, "Remember, a bottle of wine has about five or six short portions. For our crowd I think it will be safer if we get five or six of both red and white. And I'm supposed to remind you that we have our last meeting with Pastor Shannon Wednesday afternoon."

With a sheepish grin, Ward said, "Maybe we can go to the store together and you can tell me what wines we should offer." It does take a committee to come up with a working plan, doesn't it?

Lois said with a chuckle, "I'll be in charge of keeping folks lubricated."

Pastor Shannon's office was a friendly place. Ward enjoyed the art work and liturgical symbols, all of which had special meaning to her. He felt he knew her better by the things she used to decorate her study. The pastor summed up their five previous sessions by saying, "We've talked a lot about your pasts, your faith and your commitment to future growth. I'm proud of the accomplishments you have made and the responsible budgeting you have. You've given me a cursory outline of the wedding ceremony you anticipate. Tell me why you have suggested that it should be relatively brief."

Before Ward could answer, Becky said, "We will be standing on the sky patio. Our guests will not be comfortably seated. By design," her smile warmed, "brevity is gracious. We do not expect lengthy observation or explanations. I hope for a sweet memorable service. There will be no special music or readings, except Romans 12: 9 -13, which will be read by my Maid of Honor."

"Ward, does that plan feel comfortable to you?," the pastor asked with a steady gaze.

"Pastor Shannon," he answered, "this will be the first wedding I have ever attended, so I may have a different orientation than most. Frankly, if we are promising to live together as wife and husband, and are exchanging rings to seal that covenant and are pronounced newlyweds, I think the appropriate ritual might be brief."

"Ward, you have never attended a wedding of any sort?" the pastor asked incredulously.

"Pastor Shannon, I had an unkind family history and no opportunity to be exposed to social civility." Ward did not want this moment to become confronting, so he tried to be humorous. "I think Becky has a fair vision of what would be most appropriate for us. I also think she is eager to get to the champagne toast."

That made the pastor chuckle and say, "Fair enough. You want a brief ceremony, it will be so." Then recalling another subject, she asked. "Ward, Becky told me that you are registered as a Marriage Clerk with the county. Are you going to officiate weddings in your home?"

"At the moment it is only one wedding." Ward said confidently. "A close colleague at Roosevelt has asked me if I will do it for them. I don't foresee another."

"Could you use a book of Rituals of the APC that is American Presbyterian Church?"

Ward thought that was a gracious offer. "Yes, having a script to follow would be a great help. I'll bring it back to you."

Pastor Shannon sighed, "No, Ward, it's a gift. It belonged to a very dear friend in seminary." She presented Ward with a small leather bound book that showed little wear. In the fly leaf he found the name Roberto Gonzales. "He would delight to know his book is lighting the way for someone new."

Becky was listening to the tender tone of the pastor's voce. She asked softly, "By any chance, did this belong to the Bob in your Easter sermon?" Her steady gaze held Shannon's.

"You have a good memory, Becky," she said softly. "We were to be married as soon as I graduated from seminary."

Ward placed the book back on her desk as though it might be fragile. "You mustn't give me this. It is a precious memory."

She shook her head gently and said, "Some memories may be held, and some may be held in the heart. I have met another wonderful man and I believe it is time to part with things that might complicate future growth." Her shy smile was one of hope.

Becky's gaze held Ward's as she pondered where she had heard him use those tender words before and then she remembered Sophie's sadness when Silvia died and Ward's thoughtful memory gift.

Before they left the pastor's office they made sure she knew about the open house next Saturday. It would be an opportunity for her to meet the wedding party and the unusual venue.

Saturday morning awoke to a foggy gray day but the weather forecast was for a sunny afternoon. Sophie was happy to spend some time with Nana Nora who was good for two or three Chinese checker games. The guests arrived in two waves, Those related to the school board were prompt, or a couple minutes early. It took a while for some of the teachers to realize that Dr. Anthony and Kathleen were just as down to earth and impressed as all the rest. When he shared the account of Ward directing a police officer to scold him, there was laughter and new respect for those concerned.

The Republicans arrived an hour later. Dr. Jameson and Peggy enjoyed renewing their friendship with several of the educators. It was surprising to see Peggy and Kathleen share a warm embrace. As each person was welcomed, the hosts were happy to guide them through the delightful home. Lois assumed the kitchen duties and hospitality was abundant. Every visitor would claim a different highlight, until they stepped out onto the sky patio. The closeness and panorama of the lake was mesmerizing. After a few minutes, however, they seemed to congregate in the spacious family room with windows that also overlooked the lake. Lois was attentive to refresh the wine glasses there and the Bose system was playing a smooth jazz background. It seemed like an elegant movie set. More than once Ward was asked, "and you get to live here?"

The Republicans, while appreciating the amenities upstairs, where more focused on the commons and the offices they would share. "Oh this is so much better than I had hoped. We can host a large crowd here!" was heard more than once. "The amenities are perfect!" was heard even more often. Before she left, Mrs. Murphy made an appointment to meet with Ward to plan their first neighborhood event.

Three realtor-led groups wanted to tour the house and were gently told that it was a private open house and definitely not for sale. The fourth group felt they had the right to push in anyway, until they heard the heavy barking of a very large dog. Ward smiled at their hurried exit, believing that it was the best doorbell he had ever heard.

Little by little the crowd dwindled until there were just three couples and Lois. She was sipping a glass of Merlot and exclaiming how enjoyable the folks had been. "It was like a party," she said happily.

Kathleen asked Becky, "I understand you are a counselor for the district. Are you pretty busy these days?"

"Officially, I'm a Testing Psychologist," Becky answered with a comfortable smile. "I help gifted children find a more productive environment, or challenged children a more supportive one. We have about a dozen testing tools to maximize a child's learning experience." Then with a bit of a shrug, she added, "We are seldom busy, but there are always folks waiting to find the ideal situation," She was afraid there might be more questions so she asked, "Tell me how you spend your work day."

Kathleen chuckled, "It is nothing as interesting as working with children or dispensing Tootsie Rolls." Her smile was radiant. "I'm a law partner in my father's firm. We practice Corporate Compliance. A couple days each month I'm in Olympia at the Attorney General's offices. Believe me I would be much more gratified working with children. Some of the time it feels like I am but they are only old ones." Everyone chuckled.

Becky asked, "By any chance do you run into Sally Peterson there? Ward and I met them at a brunch last year."

"I do know Sally, and Peggy Jameson too. They are sorority sister, but a few years ahead of me." Her smile was more serious. "They are pretty involved in Republican politics, which I try to avoid. My job is less complicated if I remain party neutral." She brightened, "But I'm not neutral about this home, setting, and sky patio! I simply can't express my wonder in it all. Ward, how on earth did you imagine this design?"

A bit embarrassed, Ward answered, "If I were gifted enough to come up with this design, I wouldn't be dispensing Tootsie Rolls. Jay, here, has a brother who is a Reno Master. It was pretty much his concept all the way. I was just permitted to say 'yes' to the opportunity."

Jay said, "Phil told me this was going to be his top reno. My gosh, I still can't believe this is the same place we visited last year. That was a nightmare and this is a dream. I'm still wondering how you pulled this off without an inheritance." His smile was pure admiration.

Florence hooked her arm with Jay's and added, "When I saw the sky patio it took my breath away. It is so elegant and open. You did say that we are on the calendar for the 28th?"

"You bet you are" Ward replied gladly. "Just remember that I must have a Marriage License to do the wedding."

Dr. Anthony was about to ask a question but Kathleen beat him to it. "Can you tell us how this works. Will you do a wedding service for just anyone?"

Ward raised his eyebrow. "That's one of those loaded questions. The easy answer is defiantly not. Our home and time are far too valuable to become a wedding mill. If they are special friends, however," he looked at Jay, "then a wedding ceremony becomes part of a lasting friendship. Jay invited me to Giggles, where I met Becky. That alone puts him in a special category. He has become a dispenser of algebra wizardry through Tootsie Rolls. So you see, I must officiate their ceremony." He paused for a breath and finished, "That is two weeks after ours when I will see how it's done." Everyone chuckled.

"But aren't there guidelines that you must adhere to, or instructions that you must follow?" she asked.

"It is my strong hunch that they are married in the eyes of the county with the application for the license, Ward explained. "There must be a three day waiting period before it is valid. I think my task is to be a signature gatherer to activate the license before witnesses. Clerk or clergy, it doesn't seem to make any difference to the county. But, yes, they must promise in the presence of witnesses that they intend to live together, as wife and husband. That is the extent of my accountability."

Dr. Anthony said quietly, "You make that sound pretty cold."

"I think it could be," Ward shrugged, "for both the clerk and the couple. I have seen sad pictures of drive-through wedding chapels in Las Vegas. That seems to take every bit of dignity and meaning away." He smiled at Jay and Florence. "But when I get to participate in something this life defining with friends who are like family, we are all blessed. And that is never cold."

Dr. Anthony replied, "As usual, you have put a positive spin on that and made me sort of envious." He didn't want to ask the next question but was too curious not to. "What is your fee?"

"Sir, my tax report is already complicated enough. I don't have a fee, but I do ask that an appropriate contribution is made to the charity of your choice. If you have none, my suggestions are the Children's Hospital or The Red Cross Disaster Fund. I would not consider making money from my best friends."

"Then will you tell me how we get on your confirmation list?" the Superintendent asked quietly. Kathleen nodded and hooked her arm with his and nodded more energetically. There was some spirited speculation.

Finally, it was just the three of them. Lois was still charmed by the attitude of the afternoon. "So many really nice people!" she said. "They were courteous and playful at the same time. I'll bet Sophie would have had a good time today."

Ward chuckled, "I'll bet she did anyway. Nora wants to spoil her just like you have."

Lois said she would pick up Sophie and fix her a simple supper, And then they were alone. Becky was comfortable on the love seat, so when Ward approached, she held up her arms in an invitation. He straddled her and slowly bent to give her a kiss. The moment was full of gladness, and affection. The kiss lingered and grew in intensity. As she pulled his body more tightly to hers, she whispered, "I'm not sure which to say, 'Don't! Stop! or Don't stop

He eased away and a bit breathlessly said, "In just seven more days we won't need to put on the controls.'" He bent to kiss her gently and said, "Becky Lover, you are my fantasy, my deepest wish. I love you all ways."

With a smile now less urgent, she said, "Ditto! I love you more with each heart beat."

Giggles advertised their Reopening with a stellar list of comedians. Appropriately, Florence emailed a reminder that tables fifteen and sixteen would be theirs if everyone was prompt. At 6:45, however, when the first of the group arrived, they found the parking lot filled and a long line of people waiting for the doors to open. There were also two Seattle Police cruisers and at least four uniformed patrol officers.

At first glance Ward was convinced that there were already more people waiting than the seating capacity. He saw Jay and Florence near the end of the line and rolled down his window to say, "Let us get some pizza for the house. We have enough hospitality to go around. Come on over to Winter Place when the others get here." Jay waved his understanding and a new era of fellowship began.

Everyone gathered on the sky patio first. Watching the activity around the lake was enjoyable and feeling so private was pleasing. When Becky brought the three pizzas it was a delight to find that the dining room table had seating for twelve. It was like they were meant to be all together. The wine was adequate but Ward and Becky preferred diet coke. Laughter and conversation continued until nearly ten o'clock. Finally, Maria asked Sam if he would take her home, it was after all still a school night, with just one more week before summer break. They all agreed, but added that this was tons more enjoyable than Giggles. They pitched in enough cash to pay for a repeat next Thursday when instead of stand-up, they would share their summer plans.

The morning news was shocking! It reported another violent evening at Giggles. A number of gang members from the Rainier Valley, identified as the Dreads, had opened fire on their rivals from the International District, identified as the Rouge (Red). Ambulances had transferred several casualties with life-threatening injuries, to Harborview Hospital. Four of those injured were bystanders. The club has been closed indefinitely and Mayor Curtis Royer appointed a special police unit to investigate the growing gang problem.

Ward phoned the date night folks to remind them that it was his turn and he had something special in mind. They were all invited to Winter Place because the Olive Garden could provide a take-out feast for them.

When folks arrived they were surprised that Ward had set the big table in the dining room. Each person had their assigned place. Obviously he had taken some thought arranging this. Ward poured glasses of wine, and 7UP for Sophie. "I hope this works out as well as it has in my mind," their host said. "You probably heard the news from Giggles night before last. Two of the fatalities were Vietnamese from Chaney. I have no assurance that their names were Tran, but it made me so very aware of my great good fortune. Tonight is one of gratitude for the family you all have created."

He looked at Nick and Lois. "Nick you have been a welcome part of this family's recent development. Your heart and Lois' were running pretty low until last New Year's Eve. I think we all realized the possibility of new affection and we welcomed it. Lois the first evening Becky brought me in for an introduction I believe you were kindling our fire. You have both been a supportive influence. I lift my glass in affection. Thank you sincerely." He took a sip with them.

"Sophie, I started to fall in love with you that same evening when you wanted me to meet Silvia. Then you wanted me to meet the baby Jesus, which was even sweeter. But it was in the moment of that terrible crisis that you called me Daddy that my heart was completely yours. I love you." He lifted his glass and she followed with her soda.

"Becky, Love, I think my heart came alive the night you asked me out of the dining room at Giggles so you could tell me how much older and more complicated your life was than mine." He chuckled richly. "Each day I fall more in love with you and can only image what the next five decades will be like. The only word I can think of is 'wonderful'." He lifted his glass holding her eyes in an adoring gaze. "I love you forever." They drank together.

Turning toward Steve and Nora Ward said, "It all started when you accepted a foster child who had been bumped around a lot. That first day was the beginning for me to become a son, your son." His voice became softer and breathy. "You both have shown me what it means to be a loving family, courageous, generous, patient and ever so kind. God has blessed me through you. Here's to you both." They lifted their glasses together even though tears were freely flowing.

"This is a little unfamiliar for me," he continued after a deep breath. "Will you pray with me? Lord God, Gracious and all Giving, as we dine this night gratitude is filling our hearts. For one another, but supremely for what you have done in and for us. We thank you for this bounty tonight; we thank you for your abundant gifts. In this richness may our brokenness be healed, that we may receive your guidance for all our actions. We ask all this for your love's sake. Amen." He looked up with a smile and said, "Now let the feast begin!"

The first course was Minestrone soup and soft bread sticks. That was followed by a cheese plate and salad. Then one after another four platters of the Olive Garden's most popular entrees were served. If you only took a sample, which most folks did, multiplied by four that was a lot of food. Finally the chocolate raspberry sorbet completed the meal. Ward's happy smile suggested satisfaction with his plan because everyone else was smiling too. Before the evening was finished folks agreed to take some of the leftovers home. They would have either suppers or lunch for much of the coming week. Steve also made sure everyone was invited to McCormick's on Lake Union next Saturday for date night.

Becky stayed to help with the dishes. She needed Ward to know how tender his toasts were and how positive to each family member. She also wanted to chat about bringing some boxes of her things over tomorrow. It would be ideal if much of her necessities might already be moved when they returned from Victoria. Sunday afternoon accomplished most of what she had in mind. Sophie asked if she could sleep in her new room and was only a bit disappointed to learn that, like her mom, she would need to wait just a bit longer.

The vacation attitude was definitely in the Roosevelt air all week. It was a nostalgic time to collect year book signatures and an award assembly. Perhaps it was most tender for seniors who would say "farewell." Each of Ward's Friday students found a Tootsie Roll with a gold sticker star waiting for them. He told each class that he had chosen one special student who had surpassed his high expectations and was the most outstanding student. That student's Tootsie Roll bore a gold sticker star. Each student realized the compliment that was being paid to each and everyone personally. Curiously, there were no wrappers in the waste cans. Those tiny morsels were almost unanimously saved to become prized trophies.

Becky had kept her calendar appointment free for most of the Friday afternoon. She had some last minute shopping to finish and had invited Ward to a Red Robin supper.

They were happy to have a table near the corner which would be a bit less noisy. She reached her hand across the table for his. "Ward, I can't tell you how deliriously happy I am right now. It's like I'm in a dream. Do you feel that way?

"You bet," he said with an equal smile. "I've been counting the days for a couple months. My job, the house, and now a wedding, it's fabulous and a bit scary."

She squeezed his hand gently and asked, "What is scary about it?" Her eyes held his tenderly.

Ward's smile changed more to a shrug. "You know, the house is fabulous, yes, but it is only a house. The new job will be terrific, but it's only a job. You, on the other hand, my love, are gorgeous, warm and mysterious. I've read the books that Pastor Shannon suggested but there is a huge difference between theory and reality. Let's just say that I've waited my whole life for this moment and I'm a bit nervous." He now gave her hand the little squeeze.

Her smile was reassuring. "Let's just agree that we both have the jitters. For example, mom has urged me to get some sheer nightgown for Ocean Point. She thinks I should be alluring or something. I suppose it would be lovely, but so impractical. It's just not like me. I think we should just wear what we usually do for sleeping." She was trying to deflect a tender subject.

"Yeah," Ward agreed, happy for the shift, "as long as you don't laugh at my Spiderman shirt."

"Now that's funny," Becky chuckled. "Maybe I can find a Wonder Woman."

When their food was served they changed the subject to a wedding day check-list.

Ward said, "Sam has offered to take plenty of pictures for us and Nick has volunteered to drive us to Lake Union Air. Our flight is scheduled for 4:30."

Becky added, "Both mom and Nora are in charge of wine and cup cakes. I like that idea better than cutting a cake and feeding one another. I'm glad you felt the same way. Pastor

Shannon has offered to collect our signatures before the ceremony and she will have our Marriage license for everyone there to sign on the back. It will be like a guest registry. Can you think of anything we have missed?"

"Nope," he said cheerily. "I have a Thank You card for Pastor Shannon with a check in it. Steve has an extra key to the house and will make sure it's buttoned up when they leave. I think we are all set." He nodded his head but they were both mindful of their previous conversation and were sure that they could help each other navigate an unfamiliar experience.

Saturday Becky had a haircut and manicure in the morning. In the afternoon she brought her travel bag for their Victoria trip as well as her wedding gown that she could change into just before the ceremony. She assured Ward that she had remembered her passport, which reminded him to pack his as well. They were prepared.

The McCormick table was a window seating overlooking the marina and lake. Early evening sunset had warmed the vista beautifully for the date night crew. Obviously the anticipation of tomorrow's wedding was the center of conversation. Ward had just said that he could think of little else.

"I know what you mean," Nick said with a wider than usual smile. "It must be catching." He looked at Lois and she nodded. "The conversation of weddings has been pleasant for us too. I got an email from Jackson. He says his ship will be back in Bangor by Labor Day. He has been offered the job of Executive Officer of the Submarine Base. On top of that, Irene is coming back to Seattle too. She said five years in Puerto Rico was beginning to wear her down. She has a couple job opportunities that she's considering. She also wants some additional training in Children's treatment, but agreed she would be home in time to greet Jackson. They have both expressed joy in our plans. We've talked with Pastor Shannon, who has agreed to do the ceremony, if we just have a place. What do you think?" The question was not addressed to anyone specifically, so they all started speaking at once. The conclusion of the confusion was that the sky patio or commons would be available whenever they wanted it to be.

Lois finally said, "And I've been talking to a realtor who believes the market is red hot right now. He said there are even bidding wards that bring in more than the asking price, especially for a four bedroom home in close like mine. It will be easy to sell, probably as soon as it's listed."

As the dessert was being served, Steve said, "I know you told us no wedding gifts. So we took an offering for a Honeymoon help. We would like to pay for a supper or something fun. Since the bank had a bit of Canadian money on hand, Nora thought it might be fun for you to find something special for the house while you were there. The exchange rate is real favorable right now. The last time we were in Victoria she found a terrific leather purse that she still loves." He slid an envelope across the table to them. "At least you won't need to stop and convert your U.S. currency before you pay for a taxi." That made them all smile for different reasons. It was just another in the infinite line of loving expressions of a precious family.

As they were leaving the restaurant, Becky stepped in front of Ward and turned so she could face him. She placed her hands on his shoulders and whispered, "This is the last time I must go home with mom. Tomorrow is a wonderful new day, a new life together." She kissed him sweetly and said, "I'll bring my stuff in the morning. May I have the bathroom for a while about noon?" They both chuckled and kissed again.

Ward had trouble going to sleep. The house seemed extra empty. He tried to think of something other than the wonderful possibilities of tomorrow. Out loud he whispered, "While visions of sugar plums danced in his head." He woke early and toured the entire house inspecting for any last minute clean-up. A gray overcast morning muted the sun but the weatherman had promised it would burn off.

THE WEDDING

She arrived about 12:30, a vision of joy and affection. Her mom and Sophie came along to provide transportation. She wore brown slacks and a cream colored turtle neck. "This is my going –to-Victoria clothes that I will change back into after wearing the most wonderful wedding dress in the world!" Her eyes were dancing with happy anticipation.

By one o'clock she was ready with light make-up, off-white low heeled shoes and her mid-calf lovely dress. Ward recognized it immediately. It was the one from the secret cache they had discovered under the floor. Lois had altered it to fit her, taking in the waist and adding a lace panel to the bodice and collar. The dry Cleaners had restored its crisp original beauty. She was gorgeous! With Ward wearing tan slacks and an off-white mock turtle neck, they were a perfect pair! She had a small bouquet with two white rose buds and a bunch of baby's breath.

Sam and Maria were the first to arrive. He wanted to get several photos of them alone on the patio, which was bathed in sunlight and glorious in its elevated vista. Then, as each couple arrived they had a picture taken with the wedding couple under the arbor, which was adorned with hanging baskets of white and lavender petunias. Brad Anthony and Kathleen were once again struck be the sheer beauty of the setting. He could easily stand under the arbor with plenty of headroom. There were several photos taken of the family. By a quarter to two, Becky assured Pastor Shannon that if she had the signatures, all their guests had arrived. She could begin.

"Friends," the pastor's voice called for their attention, "let me invite you to gather 'round close. We have no PA, so I'd like you to be able to hear this lovely ceremony. Let's cuddle in close." Folks shuffled into a near circle around the two.

With an intimate voice, Pastor Shannon said, "At the beginning of our time together, let me remind you that we are here to publicly establish a home. The home is the oldest and dearest part of our life together. It existed before the Church, and before the State. It is a fundamental part of our human society. We of the Church believe that the home came into being, by and through, the authority of Almighty God, for the fulfillment and expression of our deepest human needs: to be loved, and to give love. This is therefore, a commitment not entered casually, but rather, thoughtfully, with reverence and respect for one another, and for God who calls us here, and now meets us here in this lovely setting. Into this holy moment these two come now to be joined."

She caught her breath before continuing, "Because a home exists in concert with others, drawing its meaning and strength from their prayers and loving support, let me first direct these questions to you all, family and friends, as a traditional part of this ceremony. Do you, acknowledging your joy in this marriage union, pledge your prayerful concern to Ward and Becky, vowing to give moral and spiritual support when needed, and granting them the freedom to be who they are, as they build their future life together? Will you aid in the Christian nurture of this new home? Do you bless them? I can think of no clearer sign of your affirmation than applause."

An immediate response was vigorous. Even folks who were walking around the lake looked up to see the source of it.

She turned toward Florence and said, "Hear these words from the pen of St. Paul:

"Love must be sincere," the Maid of Honor read, "Hate what is evil, cling to what is good. Be devoted to one another in brotherly love. Honor one another above yourselves. Never be lacking in zeal, but keep your spiritual fervor, serving the

Lord. Be joyful in hope, patient in affliction, faithful in prayer. Share with God's people who are in need. Practice hospitality. Bless those who persecute you; bless and do not curse. Rejoice with those who rejoice; mourn with those who mourn. Live in harmony with one another." Florence smiled in satisfaction.

Pastor Shannon turned toward Ward and asked, "Ward, will you have Becky to be your partner, lover, and friend in Christian marriage? Will you take her existence as seriously as your own? Will you love her, comfort her, grow with her in honor, whether in sickness or health, and remain faithful to her as long as you live?"

With a big smile Ward answered gently, "Yes, I will!"

She turned toward Becky and repeated the questions: "Becky, will you have Ward to be your partner, lover, and friend in Christian marriage? Will you take his existence as seriously as your own? Will you love him, comfort him, grow with him in honor, whether in sickness or health, and remain faithful to him as long as you live?"

With a tiny sigh, Becky said, "Oh, yes, I will." That made most of the listeners smile affectionately and some with tears.

Pastor Shannon shifted her gaze. "Sophie we even have a special question for you, sweetie. Will you have Daddy Ward as your very own? Will you promise to honor your father and mother always?"

Her small voice was confident as she answered, "With all my heart, I will."

Ward bent down and whispered something in Sophie's ear.

"Really?" the child burst out. "Do you mean it?"

Ward hugged her gently and said, "I really mean it."

The pastor took a deep breath as though instructing the couple to do likewise. "O.K. here is the tough stuff," she said playfully. Share the vows you have written for one another." She handed Ward a 3 x 5 card.

Ward turned toward Becky and laid his hands onto hers so he could read the card. "Becky, I love you, and I want to spend the remainder of my life as your husband." The words were soft and full of emotion. "Making you happy, and sharing in that happiness. From this day on, I promise to share my life, openly with you. Your joys are my joys; your burdens are my burdens; your prayers are my prayers." I have found you to be the partner with whom I can laugh and cry, build and grow, live and love. No matter what comes to us, I pledge you my faith, to uphold you, and live with you, in the joy of God's love."

She embraced him, then received the card, although she didn't look at it. "Ward, I love you, and I want to spend the remainder of my life as your wife, making you happy, and sharing in that happiness. From this day on, I promise to share my life, openly with you. Your joys are my joys; your burdens are my burdens; your prayers are my prayers. I have found you to be the partner with whom I can laugh and cry, build and grow, live and love. No matter what comes to us, I pledge you my faith, to uphold you, and live with you, in the joy of God's love." She leaned forward and gave him a gentle kiss.

The pastor said to those watching, "That was just a practice kiss." There were chuckles enough to regain their concentration.

"Now, where are those rings?" the pastors asked playfully. Sophie lifted a small satin pillow with the rings safely tied on a bow. "Thank you Sweetie," the pastor said as she untied them, offering the first one to Ward.

He said without her instruction, "Becky, I give you this wedding ring as a seal of our marriage. May it be a witness for the entire world to see our love! I pledge you my love as long as I live." He leaned over to kiss her gently.

Becky replied: "Ward, in receiving this ring, I receive you as my husband."

The pastor offered the other ring to Becky who said, "Ward, I give you this wedding ring as another seal of our marriage. May it be a witness for the entire world to see our love! I pledge you my love as long as I live."

Ward answered her, "Becky, in receiving this ring, I do receive you as my wife."

Pastor Shannon held their two hands and said in a stronger voice, "Because you two have consented to be joined in the holy bonds of matrimony, and have given witness to the sacredness of your vows, and your love, before God, and this gathering of your family and closest friends, because you have committed your love and loyalty to one another in sacred promises, with the giving and receiving of wedding rings, I affirm that God has joined you as wife and husband. Let all people here and everywhere recognize and respect this sacred union, now and forever more. Amen. Now, a kiss seals the covenant."

Rousing applause accompanied the kiss and those present understood that brevity did not distract from the sacred ceremony. There were four other couples who felt that this ceremony was a perfect model for their own, as soon as it could be scheduled.

Ward and Becky stepped over to the folding table where Lois and Nick were pouring glasses of wine and Steve and Nora were setting out cup cakes. Becky intentionally handed her bouquet to Florence saying, "You're next."

The newlyweds made sure they shared conversations and sips of wine with everyone. Becky loved telling the story of her dress and how it came to be used seventy five years after its purchase. Again and again they heard compliments of a most tender and uplifting wedding.

Perhaps the most pointed was from Kathleen who said, "I have attended many weddings, most of which were extravagant displays. Once again I admire the ability you have to do something simply wonderful and wonderfully simple. I have forgotten most of those other ones, but I am pretty sure we will remember this one fondly. I would rejoice at something so authentic instead of the big show. Maybe we can talk about it when you have returned from your honeymoon."

Dr. Anthony was nodding his agreement. "Congratulations for a riveting service," he said sincerely. "There was nothing cold or neglected by it. I was enthralled and am so moved by your grasp of what is important. I am a fond admirer of you both." He gave Becky a hug, and then Ward.

The celebration continued for about an hour. Then Becky excused herself to change so they could catch their Lake Union flight to Victoria. On the way there she asked Ward, "What did you say to Sophie that so thrilled her? I was a little jealous not to be in on it."

Ward chuckled, "I told her that when we get home from our vacation, we will find us a new Silvia. It seemed an appropriate promise at the time."

Becky squeezed his hand affectionately and said, "That is so like you to make sure she has a surprise thrill too. I love you forever." From the front seat Nick watched her kiss him again.

By 5:30 they were cleared through Canadian Customs and the water taxi had taken them to the Ocean Point dock. Ward asked if she would rather go up to the room first or the dining room. Shyly Becky answered, "I would rather not get dressed again this evening." The words were whispered without a blush.

What should we say about the honeymoon? You are correct, it isn't a trick question. The appropriate answer is, as little as possible. Let it be sufficed to say that for three marvelous days they found new expressions of wonder, discovery and affection.

As soon as they returned to Seattle they found a pet store that provided all the necessary things a kitten might want, including a carpeted shelter that rested on the top of Sophie's armoire and a climbing tree that would give exercise and access to it. There were two litter boxes that hopefully would be used. Sophie chose a gray and black kitten that thrilled her completely. The family laid claim to Winter Place.

The calendar filled quickly. Jay and Florence were married on June 29th. Phil was the best man and the recipient of countless praise for the renovation There were several in attendance who wanted his contact information. Florence was a radiant bride in her gown and veil. No one would guess the struggle she had in confronting a lingering ghost. She had asked Becky a tender question. "How in the world did you get over the death of your dad first, and then Jess? It's been seven years since that creep Roger derailed my life, and I am still angry about it. The grief of it twists my thinking. I'm still a little afraid to completely trust Jay. I keep thinking he is hiding something from me."

"I heard once," her friend had replied softly, "that when a deep injury is done to us, we never recover until we forgive. You can't change the past, only how you hold it in your mind. Maybe it's time for you to get Roger out of your head. Just forgive him. Say it out loud. Let it go as a sad but finalized part of your history. You'll know it's gone when you believe in Jay completely."

As Ward was making the pronouncement there was such peace and joy in their hearts that Florence knew the truth of that advice. The wedding, once again on the sky patio, was another precious expression of faith and hope. With new family members attending, the cadre of admires continued to grow.

Sam and Maria were married at 9:30 P.M. on July 4th. The fireworks launched from Duck Island in Green Lake gave an entertaining conclusion to the wedding service. All the folks in attendance agreed that Ward was an excellent Marriage Clerk, but not as spectacular as the rockets' red glare.

When Suzanne Murphy and her planning folks met for the first time Ward was given a sense of the scope of her idea. With 22 zip codes for Seattle, they would need to go on a trial basis to determine attendance. The initial invitation went out to over a thousand Republicans. It was sweetened by an offer of a 50% discount for a Hollywood Car Detailing at the Toyota dealership. Attendance was required to activate the offer. The team decided that rather than leap into an issue oriented agenda they would simply focus on patriotism and outstanding Republican office-holders currently serving

Washington State. The three minute Otto Whittaker poem "I Am America", spoken by Johnny Cash would be followed by a fifteen minute overview of the State's highlights spoken by Suzanne.

On July 13th the 3 P.M. attendance was 122 folks. Very close to capacity of the Commons room. Mrs. Murphy was delighted to use the opportunity as a springboard for a Republican rally. And even those who had heard the Whittaker essay, welcomed it again:

I Am the Nation

I was born the 4th of July 1776, and the Declaration of Independence is my birth certificate. The bloodlines of the world run in my veins, because I offered freedom to the oppressed. I am many things, and many people! I am the Nation! I am 324 million living souls, and the host of millions who have lived and died for me.

I am Nathan Hale and Paul Revere. I stood at Lexington and fired the shot heard around the world. I am Washington, Jefferson, and Patrick Henry. I am John Paul Jones, the Green Mountain boys, Davy Crockett. I am Lee, Grant, and Abe Lincoln.

I remember the Alamo, the Maine, the Pearl Harbor, and the World Trade Center. When freedom called, I answered, and stayed until it was over, over there. I left my heroic dead in Flanders Field, on the Rock of Corregidor, on the bleak slopes of Korea, in the steaming jungles of Vietnam, and the desert sands of Iraq.

I am the Brooklyn Bridge, the wheat fields of Kansas, and the granite hills of Vermont. I am the coalfields of the Virginias and Pennsylvania, and the fertile lands of the west, the Golden Gate, and the Grand Canyon. I am Independence Hall, the Monitor, and the Merrimac.

I am big! I sprawl from the Atlantic to the Pacific...my arms reach out to embrace Alaska and Hawaii...three million square miles throbbing with industry. I am more than three million farms. I am forest, field, mountain, and desert. I am quiet villages in the country, and teeming cities that never sleep.

You can look at me and see Ben Franklin walking down the streets of Philadelphia with his bread-loaf under his arm. You can see Betsy Ross with her needle. You can see the lights of Christmas, and hear the strains of "Auld Lang Sine" as the calendar turns to a fresh year.

I am Babe Ruth and the World Series. I am 130,000 schools and colleges, and 326,000 churches where my people worship God as they think best. I am a ballot dropped in a box, the roar of a crowd in a stadium, and the voice of a choir in a cathedral. I am the editorial in a newspaper, and a letter to a congressman.

I am Eli Whitney and Stephen Foster. I am Tom Edison, Albert Einstein, and Billy Graham. I am Horace Greely, Will Rogers, and the Wright brothers. I am George Washington Carver, Daniel Webster, and Jonas Salk. I am Longfellow, Harriet Beecher Stowe, Walt Whitman, and Thomas Paine.

Yes, I am the nation, and these are the things that I am. I was conceived in freedom and, God willing, in freedom will I spend the rest of my days.

May I possess always the integrity, the courage and the strength to keep myself unshackled, to remain a citadel of freedom, and a beacon of hope to the world."

Otto Whittaker

The first neighborhood gathering was seen as a great success for all concerned. Even Steve reported that of the twenty folks who took advantage of the detailing, ten of them who heard how much their car would bring as a trade in, decided to take advantage of an attractive Toyota deal.

Ward recognized the car that parked by the commons door. He went downstairs immediately to greet Kathleen Hall. "Becky and Sophie are helping Lois get her house ready for sale," he said cordially, yet telling her that he was here alone.

"That's just as well Ward," she replied and he could tell she had been weeping. "I realize you are not a priest or a therapist, but I need your counsel and your confidential ear." Her gaze was steady and concerned.

"Kathleen, friend, tell me how I can help you." Ward was sure his listening skill was about to be tested. He invited her into the office with windows that faced the parking lot. It was less private than some of the other rooms.

"You might guess," she began slowly, "that Brad and I have been extremely close and happy about our relationship." She took a ragged breath. "I think since he has met you, he has a model that he would like to incorporate. He really likes you," she paused a moment and added, "and so do I. I trust you, which is something new for me."

Ward asked again with a concerned voice, "What may I do to help you?"

"You already are listening," she said a bit brighter. "My people don't do that very well. They often leap to conclusions and I do too." She sat up more erect and lifted her chin. "I found Bradley's desktop calendar and made a frightening discovery, On a Friday in May, there is an entry that says Sandy D7 $10,000. The next Friday says, 'Easy Lovin'." Another sob tried to make its way out. "Then every Friday afternoon in June was blocked off. I have no knowledge of any appointments he had and am left with the conclusion that it might be clandestine. Her name, address, and price." Now a shudder came with the sob.

Ward moved close enough to her to place his hand on her shoulder. "Yes, that sounds like a possible explanation." He shook his head saying, "But it doesn't sound credible for the man I know him to be. He loves and respects you. And right along with that thought is your sense of self-worth. You are quite lovely, intelligent and successful. That doesn't seem like a formula for infidelity. Do you think there might be some other possibilities?"

"What else could 'easy lovin" mean?" Her voice was raised in volume and pitch.

"I don't know," he answered softly. "Has there ever been a hint of his unhappiness in your relationship, any inappropriate interest in other women?"

"No. never," she said softly. "But I don't know what else it could be. There is always a first time." She shook her head sadly.

"Let's think about that a bit, Kathleen." Ward thought for a moment and then offered, "It could be the name of a song, or a play," he intentionally chuckled. "It could be the name of a wine or a race horse or a reclining chair. For sure there are any number of explanations that would not be so hurtful". He took a moment to phrase his next question. "Did you say anything to him about your fear?"

"Oh heavens no," she whispered. "That might wreck everything."

Ward gave her shoulder a gentle squeeze. "It seems you are already suffering as though that has happened."

She reached up and gave his hand a gentle pat. "You're right. I am." It seemed like a surprise to her. "What do you think I should do?"

"Kathleen, I think you should talk with Brad. You don't need to tell him the hurtful conclusion you leaped to, because that implies some distrust. You know, guys often get into perfectly acceptable stuff before they have thought it through completely. At the wedding I told Sophie we could get her a new kitten. I hadn't said a word about that to Becky. It just seemed like a good idea at the time."

"Is that what you whispered to Sophie?" Now a stronger smile found a reason.

"Yes, Becky had to ask me on the way to Victoria," he confessed. "But when she learned the truth of it she knew that it was done in love for her daughter and everything was terrific." He looked at her carefully. "As marvelous, intelligent and talented as your Brad is, I'll bet he could get the cart before the horse real easily. It's just a guy thing." There was another moment of thought. "Can you imagine that he has done something very wonderful, something super romantic for you that he wants to keep a secret until you are married?"

"That's not the Bradley way, I'm afraid. But yes, I can imagine that. It changes the picture, doesn't it?" A braver smile appeared. "That's a whole lot more pleasant to imagine than where I was a few minutes ago."

"Friend, remember that I am a real amateur at this sort of thing. My track record is still in progress. But I do believe that if you can ask him a question without hurtful accusation or attack, he will tell you the whole truth and nothing but the truth. And if you two want to come back and chat with us, you are always welcome here." He helped her stand and she tenderly embraced him.

"Ward, I can't tell you what a saint you are," she said softly. "I came in here just a few minutes ago all riled up; forgotten were my skills and training. In what, fifteen minutes? You have put my feet back down on solid ground. I so appreciate you. May I offer some compensation for your time?"

Ward snorted, "Now that's funny! I hope we become even better friends so that we would never need to think about that. Maybe we can share a meal together soon."

It was almost 9:00 when the phone rang. Ward answered politely.

"Hey Ward," he heard Brad's voice. "I hope I'm not keeping the newlyweds up." He chuckled and added, "I just have to thank you for the intervention with Kathleen. We've been talking about it for the whole evening. She told me how upset she was and I can see how she might jump to a wrong conclusion. But she also told me how calm you were and how comforting. I want you to know this was definitely not a personnel exercise. You did us a great favor today, and you were pretty spot on. I have been making a purchase that will thrill her. Yeah, it's lots bigger than a kitten." He paused for a breath and Ward thought he might be hesitant to share the truth.

"Her family has been big in boating in California. 'Easy Lovin' is a 47 foot Bayliner Pilot House Cruiser. It's a bank repo and I had to get a fellow named Sandy from the boatyard to go up to Nanaimo to bring it back for refurbishing. I've been taking a Coast Guard course every Friday afternoon. I'm becoming proficient in boat handling and management. Now that the kitten is out of the bag, so to speak, I can get really excited about it. I just didn't want you to think poorly of me. I'm hoping you folks will be willing to go out some with me. I need a crewman to help me dock her. Am I still in your good graces?"

"Brad I hope you know that I am a steadfast fan of yours. I hope Kathleen told you that I can imagine dozens and dozens of explanations that a frightened wife might not think of first."

"She told me that you were outstanding in my defense. That's why I wanted to call this evening, to thank you again. You helped us begin a conversation I was a bit hesitant to introduce. She is at least as thrilled about the purchase as I am. Aren't we strange creatures?"

"I'm super happy for you both," Ward said warmly. "And while I may need to refresh my knots and splices, I'm sure we would love an introduction to 'Easy Lovin'".

"You've got a standing invitation. She'll be in the boatyard a couple more weeks, mainly getting fresh paint, some fresh upholstery and the engines tuned. Good night, good friend and thanks again. We'll talk a bunch more later."

As he was going upstairs to chat with Becky, he smiled knowing that many wives believe owning a boat is not much different than having a mistress.

The third neighborhood gathering was another success. Folks had been filled with patriotism and Suzanne was sure there were several new volunteers identified. Now that everyone had gone, Ward's task was clean-up. He was wearing some pretty grubby work clothes. The folding chairs had to be placed on the dollies and wheeled into the storage room. He was just running the vacuum when he heard the dog bark door bell. As he shouted for Magic to knock it off, he was aware of a fellow who had not been doing so well. His clothes were dirty and worn. His hair and beard were unkempt. Ward opened the door and asked, "What can I do for you, Dude?"

"Does Wart Winter live here?" the man mumbled.

"Did you say Wart? There isn't anyone here with that name." Ward was on full alert because he was sure of this guy's identity and could see the wreckage of some tough times.

"Yeah, well, his name is Ward and he's my brother. I've been lookin' all over hell for him. He borrowed money from me and I want it back. Does he live here?" He was neither aware of his condition or the person to whom he was speaking.

Ward said, "Hey Dude, does this look like somebody's house. This is a clinic, yeah, an HIV clinic." He was studying the person in front of him and could not recognize his memory of a brother.

"But the sign says 'Winter Place. I'm Michael Winter. Now tell me if my brother lives here." His voice was a bit raised with his frustration. "I need my money, quit jerkin' me around." He started to push his way in.

"I wouldn't go in there if I were you," Ward warned as he stepped out of the way. "There is a lot of contamination, you know AIDS, man."

The confused man stopped with those words. It was likely that he was in some sort of drug event. He looked around and asked again, "Does my brother live here?"

"No Dude! Nobody lives here! I told you it's a clinic where people come to die. You know, spring time, summer, fall and winter, the end." He shook his head as though it was tragic.

The shabby figure sagged in another hopeless moment. He finally turned and shuffled back out the door. "But he owes me money," he mumbled.

"I've got a few dollars I could give you. That would get you into the Mission or Salvation Army. But Dude, you've got to be careful." He looked around warily. "If the cops catch you pan handling on private property you'll go to jail again sure as hell.'"

Michael held out his hand, waiting for some pay-off. "How much you got?"

Tears were in Ward's eyes. This was a scene he hoped he could soon forget. He was sure however that this heartbreaking moment would remain in his memory. "Here's a twenty Dude. If I ever see you around the clinic again, I'll call the police. Do you understand?"

The shell of what once was a brother took the money and turned away saying, "Whatever."

Ward wanted to scold him, shout after him to get his life in order, to warn him of the disastrous road he was on. But he did none of that. Michael had chosen his path again and again over the years. They might have the same DNA but that was the only commonality between the two men. He was careful to say nothing about the episode to Becky. Yet, for three days he thought of it often and he wondered if he had it to do over…. He was sure there were better options than the one he chose.

Monday afternoon he was studying when his phone rang. The caller identified himself as Doug Hall Jr. "I've just been in a business meeting with a mutual friend. She has asked me to give you a call. By any chance may I stop by your office? I'm on my way back to Pasadena in a couple hours."

For clarity, Ward asked, "You'd like to come over now?"

"If that is not too much of an inconvenience," he said. "I'll only take a few minutes of your time and I promise not to try to sell you anything." There was a happy chuckle that caused Ward to smile

"Then come on over, by all means. Do you know how to find me?"

"My colleague is familiar with the area and is taking me to the airport. She assures me that we won't be lost or long."

Twenty minutes later Ward recognized the car and the driver. Kathleen Hall was bringing him a puzzle. He went downstairs to meet them. "Mr. Hall, you have a distinguished chauffer," he said in greeting. He shook Mr. Hall's hand, but shared a hug with Kathleen. "Tell me what I can do for you folks today," he cheerily added. He led the way upstairs to the spacious family room where Becky and Sophie added their greetings.

When everyone was seated, Mr. Hall said, "I won't take much of your time today. She probably hasn't shared with you that Kathleen is the great granddaughter of Joyce Hall, founder of Hallmark Cards, and yes as Doug Hall Jr. I am attached to the same marvelous tree. I'm CEO of Crown Media Holdings. Kathleen has told me a bit of your amazing story. She has been singing praise of your wedding since I arrived. And your practical counseling skills were very much appreciated. I wonder if I could interest you in writing an account of your life journey to date. I envision a manuscript of about a hundred standard pages. Hallmark can't publish every story we receive, but we do pay $100 per page for an opportunity to preview one of such diverse interest under contract. We also need it in a timely fashion so we would hope for a printable copy within six months. Does that interest you at all Ward?"

When Ward only looked at Becky and then Kathleen, Mr. Hall added, "I only promised not to try to sell you something. I do believe I'm trying to buy a delightful story of achievement and affection.

Ward finally answered, "I am overwhelmed that Hallmark might find interest in my story. But, yes, I would be delighted to do that. I can start on that right away."

Kathleen opened her large purse to produce a signed contract. "This commits Crown Media to meet the agreement we have just outlined," she said in a business voice. "With your signature, you give us full rights to the work and freedom to edit for content or time allotment." Before he could ask, she said, "No we never change facts. There might be an enhancement here or there, but very little editing. We want it to be your story." She offered him a pen to sign both copies and just that simply Ward was on a fresh path. "Do you think we could take Uncle Doug up to the sky patio before we leave?"

Ward thought about the challenge for hours that evening. It wasn't the only thing on his mind of course. He thought about it as he awoke and again after breakfast, Finally, by mid morning, Becky said simply, "Just start somewhere interesting. I remember Dr. Bob telling me that if I just get one sentence written, I would be half done."

Ward opened a fresh Word document. He titled it, "The Effect of Tootsie Rolls." He stared at the screen for several minutes before he wrote:

"I guess it all started with a gray kitten named Silvia.

Seattle traffic is never pleasant. Summer Friday afternoons might be the very worst time to be in a hurry. The Toyota courtesy van had picked up a passenger at Northgate and was in route to the downtown dealership. Just before the Aurora Bridge the blue Ford in front of him hit her brakes and came to a full stop. A young woman sprang from the driver's door oblivious of the many cars that were coming to a panic stop. She was an unexpected obstacle.

"What the hell, Lady! Get back in your car for crying out loud!" He honked his horn vigorously. A couple cars behind him joined in the noise. Strangely the young woman just waved and pointed toward the curb. Her wide smile seemed incongruous to the situation.

"Get in the car fool!" he said impatiently. "Do you have a brain in that thick skull?" They were words that had been growled at him as a child.

The blue Ford driver bent down and scooped up a tiny gray kitten. She had seen the car in front of her throw the hapless creature onto the busy street without slowing down. She ran back to her car door waving the rescued feline so the other drivers could see the reason for her action. A couple drivers honked approvingly."

Finis: The Effect of Tootsie Rolls

Printed in the United States
By Bookmasters